Women Writing Letters
celebrating the art
Seasons 3 & 4

Tara Goldstein

Amanda Greer

EDITORS

Gailey Road Productions
Toronto

First published in 2015 by
Gailey Road Productions
E-mail: gaileyroad@gmail.com
Web: www.gaileyroad.com

Cover and book design by Lisa Rupchand
ISBN 978-1-312-81904-7

To our writers,
With many thanks for your stories and support of
Women Writing Letters.

To our Gailey Road Women Writing Letters
Production Team Margot Huycke, Sarah O'Sullivan,
Emma Smith and Edlyn Wong,

With many thanks for your enthusiasm and commitment to
Women Writing Letters

CONTENTS

SEASON 4

INTRODUCTION

Dear Readers,

In your hands is not simply a book, meaning it is not simply a collection of pages bound together with string and glue to be bought and sold, passed on from secondhand bookshops to Christmas stockings to dusty bookshelves. What you're holding goes beyond the tangible. What you're holding are memories, fleeting emotions, moments captured, and moments lost. What you're holding are letters, written from the deepest places of their authors' minds, the places where humour, anxiety, despair, and trepidation mingle together to form something indescribably human.

Welcome to *Women Writing Letters, Volumes 3 & 4.*

As Lord Byron once said, "Letter writing is the only device for combining solitude with good company." What he means, of course, is that a letter cannot exist without a recipient. Each of the extraordinarily talented writers in this volume have used their letters to address those important to them in their lives, be it a lost family member, an old flame, or someone who deserves to know how much their life means to someone else.

The writers have also, in a way, addressed their letters to you.

You, the readers, have been invited to share in the writers' solitude, to peek into their lives for a few hundred words.

By extending their hands to you, these writers have shown incredible strength. They have translated their experiences and heartbreak into language, and shared that language with you all. Thank you to all the writers who contributed to this anthology. Thank you for sharing your moments.

As correspondence today more or less constitutes short, quippy text messages, or pithy Twitter posts, the art of letter writing is viewed as just that—an art (albeit a lost one). These writers have ensured and proven that letters are not a dying art, but rather an evolving art, an art that, though perhaps no longer used for marriage proposals and love affairs, are used to work through painful experiences, to say the things that were too hard to say at the time, to finally banish phantom grievances.

These writers have proven that letters really do combine solitude with good company.

I hope you enjoy *Women Writing Letters, Volumes 3 & 4*.

Sincerely,
Amanda Greer

SEASON 3: PART ONE

A LETTER TO THE TEACHER I'LL NEVER FORGET
October 27, 2013

Joan Burrows

Beverley Cooper

Joan Green

Marcia Johnson

Carolyn Peters

A Letter to the Teacher I'll Never Forget

by
Joan Burrows

Dear...Miss McGrade,

I'm smiling as I begin this letter because I'm wondering if you would've caught that little falter in the salutation. I wanted to start with "Dear Betty," as if we were old friends, old acquaintances, women now of a certain age who could address each other so informally and so casually. But I couldn't. Even after all these years, to me, you are always Miss McGrade.

I'm still in touch with your family. As a kid, I remember I played baseball every summer at Holly Park with your nephews, and I thought how lucky they were that they had you for their aunt. Years later, one of them married my best friend's sister. And lately, there've been family showers and weddings. But you haven't been able to attend.

It would've been nice if you had. It would've been so nice to sit and reminisce, talk together about being teachers. Instead, I'm writing you this letter because you are the one I will never forget.

Thinking back to my elementary school years, I can recall magic moments such as reading for the first time, learning to print, turning those straight lines into cursive writing, and the thrill of using a cartridge fountain pen for the first time. But I can honestly say, Miss McGrade, that I remember everything you taught us in our grade six classroom.

For social studies that year, I had a pink Hilroy three-ringed notebook, and my first page was all about...Ponce de Leon.

Who? A Spanish explorer.

What? He sailed through the Caribbean and found Florida.

<u>When?</u> Early 1500's.

<u>Why?</u> He was looking for the fountain of youth. (And isn't that why we still all go to Florida today?).

<u>How?</u> Well, this was usually a hand drawn map with arrows of where he started from and where he ended up.

Each page of that pink three-ringed notebook had the same pattern for all of those early explorers: Vasco de Gama, Magellan, Sir Francis Drake. And the ones who came to Canada— Jacques Cartier got two full pages, and Samuel de Champlain, well he had three. I remember my favourites were Radisson and Grosseilliers not because of what they did – something about the northwest passage – but because I just liked the sound of their names together. (Plus, I could always spell Grosseilliers). I loved my social studies notebook. It was so easy to study from: say the question, use your hand to cover the answer, peek if you had to—history was suddenly so easy.

Geography that year was all about Australia. And we learned everything about it: the states and the capitals, the koalas and kangaroos, sheep shearing, how their seasons were opposite to ours, their funny words, like swagman, billabong, jumbuck. I can still sing all the words to *Waltzing Mathilda*…"and he sang as he watched and waited for his billy boil"…that's tea. It has come in handy when rocking children to sleep. For years, I dreamed of going to Australia because of you. I finally did and it was exactly as you had promised.

In arithmetic that year, we learned how to add with decimal points. At the end of the term, you sat at your desk and ordered, "O.K. birds, take our your arithmetic notebooks." And then you proceeded to call out a series of numbers: 74.5, 82, 91.5, and so on. We added them up as fast as we could and then divided to find the percentage. It took us a while to realize that we were actually figuring out our own marks for the report cards. No calculators in those days. Just busy students. But I do remember that when an impressive mark was scored, you'd look at that student and give them a wink. That was the year I came first in the class.

But what I remember most, Miss McGrade, were the readings after lunch. We'd hurry up the stairs, hang up our coats in that old musty cloak room and settle with our heads in our hands for a short story or a poem. Our favorite was always *Little Baptiste*—the way you would recite it with a French Canadian accent...and you weren't even French Canadian! Your grandfather voice made us cry every time.

Then one day, you introduced us to Anne Shirley. The first time you held up *Anne of Green Gables*, we were aghast at the size of the book. Never would we be able to get through it. But each day, we'd beg, "More!" as you finished a chapter. Anne was one powerful character. She weaned me away from my Nancy Drews. I couldn't wait for you to finish the book. So I had to get my own copy out of the town library and then I had to read all of the other Anne books in the series. My head was buried for the rest of the year.

In those days, Public Hydro sponsored a yearly public speaking contest for grades six to eight. One of the topics was, "My Favourite Character in Fiction." Well, what else could I do? You had made Anne so real to me. I'd never been in a public speaking contest before, and although I was terrified, I tried very hard to mimic the way you would say, "Oh, Marilla!" The judges laughed. I came in second. When I proudly brought back my little trophy to show you, you asked, "So what was the first place speech about?"

"A boy spoke about someone named Albert Schweitzer," I replied.

You put your hands on my shoulders, and lamented, "Oh, kiddo, you didn't stand a chance against Schweitzer."

My year in your class was breathtaking for me. I had never soared so high before or probably since. Your expectation for all of us to think better, do better, just be better people was contagious. You'd stride down George St. and onto the playground, carrying your little brown handbag at your side, the one that I accidentally saw open one day on your desk and was aghast to see a McDonald Export cigarette package, the one with the Scottish girl in her tartan. My mother couldn't even smoke those. And once on the playground, you'd gather all the girls in your class and demand, "Play together!" So there was tall, awkward, skinny me turning rope for the girls with the teased hair and black leather jackets that reeked of, well to be blunt, your McDonald exports. But all of us were laughing together despite our differences.

It takes a special kind of confidence to demand such behaviour from children. And you just naturally had it. Your power over us came not only from your own strength of character but also from your humour, your sense of fairness and equality, and your ability to make us forget about ourselves and actually be interested in the world. Not an easy task when dealing with 11-year-olds.

I have not forgotten our last visit. Arrangements were made with your sister to see you in your new home. The assisted living building loomed large as we approached. On our drive over, I listened as your sister shared with me the story of your decline. At first, the seemingly unimportant forgetfulness, of names, places, simple tasks, and then, the onset of sudden violent explosions of words and hands. There was the day you managed to escape the house, a door left unlocked. How she panicked at where you'd gone or what might've happened to you. Hours later, a hefty policeman arrived with his hand firmly on the arm of a somewhat confused-looking old lady only to find out she wasn't Miss McGrade. When you were eventually found, the outcome was inevitable—a place with locked doors.

The day we visited, I feared that you might not remember me. But you did. Forty some years since we had last seen each other. I told you I had become a teacher and was now retired and working on being a writer. You were so pleased. "I taught her," you said to the others in the lounge. You toured me through your room, your floor, and when passing through one area, showed disdain for those who were folding towels. "They asked me to fold laundry when I came here. But I'm not doing that," you said. And I agreed with you. Who wants to fold laundry? I've heard since, however, that this is something you now do.

When we were leaving, your sister warned me that you would hold on. You would take a wrist and you would want to come down the elevator. Unclasping your hand that afternoon was wretched. If only I could've freed you, taken you back to

8

who you once were, given you the liberty to be an explorer of life once more.

    <u>Who?</u> You, Miss McGrade.

    <u>When?</u> 1964.

    <u>What?</u> Best teacher ever.

    <u>Why?</u> Because...you just were!

    And the <u>How?</u> My map of you, Miss McGrade, would seem endless. It would fill, at the very least, an entire notebook.

    Thank you so much.

Sincerely,
Joan Burrows,
Grade Six Class of 1964.

A Letter to the Teacher I'll Never Forget

by
Beverley Cooper

Sometimes, if I concentrate, I can bring my mind back inside the body of my teenaged self; I can feel the painful eczema peeling away the skin on my hands, my long, straight hair hiding acne on my cheeks. I feel the soft pink sweater I liked to wear over my too-small breasts. And I can see out through my wire-rimmed glasses to the world I inhabited back then: the wide, dim corridors of Sir Winston Churchill Secondary School. Two thousand students culled from an assortment of cultures and classes. Coming from a very small, bland elementary school of roughly 200 kids, high school felt overwhelmingly intimidating.

On my first day of high school, after much agonizing deliberation, I wore the pink sweater, along with purple corduroy stovepipe pants, matching bolero vest and North Star running shoes. My mother had sewed the vest and pants based on a Butterick pattern, which was not very cool, but I held hope that I would blend in with the crowd.

I couldn't find my locker. I didn't know anyone in my classes. The other girls seemed assured and aloof. The boys friendly but impossibly immature. Between fourth period and fifth periods, while looking for the way to gym class, I wound up in the cavernous cafeteria. A grade twelve student, who, judging by his gargantuan size and bushy red facial hair, was clearly already a man, came up to me, his arms spread wide, shouting for the benefit of his friends, "Hey baby, where you been all my life?!" Guffaws spewed from his cohorts. In my mortified state, I knew:

fitting in was not going to come easy. Humiliation could be the name of the game.

Madame Auders attempted to teach me French. Not Quebecois French, which she believed to be inferior to the romantic lyricism of the Parisian accent. She was a tiny bleached blonde woman, perpetually tippy-toed, perching on her high heels. Her make-up thick and bright, her teaching style harsh and cruel. I gulped back tears as Madame Auders scorned my attempts at verb conjugations.

My math teacher, young and inexperienced, had a nervous habit of picking his nose and flicking it randomly out over his audience. My English teacher believed Ouija Boards were tools of the devil. My science teacher, angry at Wilfred Woo's minor misbehavior, wacked the poor boy's hands with a ruler that had a cutting edge, slicing the skin on Wilfred's hand, blood bursting forth.

I quickly realized that high school was something that had to be navigated very carefully; injuries were everywhere, both physical and emotional.

As a younger human, I loved playing games of pretend. There was an unused room on the second floor of our house, with a sink and no heat, where I set up an elaborate doll world. I would beg my friends to go to the empty lot to play out adventure fantasies. By myself, I would play a game called "Aunt Polly" in which I was an orphan and nasty Aunt Polly was raising me. She banned me from the house, forcing me to live under the back deck and fend for myself in the "wilds" of my suburban Vancouver backyard. These flights of imagination allowed me to escape the mundane and the hurtful, giving me the chance to dream up stories which I could shape as I chose. I reluctantly gave up these games of pretend when I started high school, but only because I was afraid of being ridiculed.

At some point during that first week at Churchill Secondary, when I thought I might have to transfer to Siberia, I found out that there was a class in make-believe. It was called drama and it was taught by Mrs. Norman. Fran Norman. A teacher who, quite simply, changed the course of my life.

During that first year, I circled Mrs. Norman's world as much as I could. I joined the choir, which she ran like a captain sailing the Royal Britannia. There I learned about something called high standards; Mrs. Norman's husband was an opera singer; her son made his living writing music; she hung out with professional luminaries like Dame Joan Sutherland and Brent Carver. She expected discipline from all of her students and wouldn't accept anything less. Our choir sang the Hallelujah Chorus and Vivaldi and madrigals, working every note to perfection. I learned from Mrs. Norman that the arts were not to be taken lightly, but were a kind of devotion.

But it was drama that really fascinated me, and eventually, in grade 10, I managed to get into Mrs. Norman's class. Suddenly, my world opened up to the brilliant possibilities of theatre. A world where I could slip out of my insecure self and slip on accents, costumes, make-up and whole other personalities. A world where I could write plays, cast them, star in them and produce them. My acting was broad and raw, but Mrs. Norman impressed upon me that theatre wasn't a place to show off; acting was inhabiting the world of a play and sharing that world with an audience.

Mrs. Norman directed two big shows a year, a musical and a play. Twice a year I auditioned, yearning to see my name on the list of successful thespians but it wasn't until grade 12, when I when I worked on my audition with dedication that would have made Daniel Day-Lewis proud, that I was cast in the part of Lucy in *You're a Good Man Charlie Brown*. And, on opening night, when every inch of me believed I was that bossy girl who needed to organize poor Charlie Brown, when I was drunk with the audience's laughter and applause; I wasn't that insecure girl of grade eight, but was in a place where I belonged. I found my spiritual home in the theatre, and it was Mrs. Norman who guided me there.

A Letter to the Teacher I'll Never Forget

by
Joan Green

Dear Sister Conrad,

I was at a party one evening, and the conversation turned to what makes school engaging for kids. Discussions about schools and schooling have been a pretty regular part of my life for over forty years, so I am rarely at a loss for words at these moments. However, this occasion was a little different; instead of being called upon to defend the publicly funded education system to someone with a cocktail in hand and a belligerent viewpoint about education's failures, I was invited to think about a teacher who had really made a difference for me.

The person who asked was interested in the kind of interactions that touched the core of young people and stood the test of time, if only in memory.

It took only a moment for me to begin thinking about you and that Grade 11 year at St. Joseph's High School, when you made such a profound impression on me. Not the kind of impression that led me to consider a religious vocation, you understand—ironically, it was your capacity to relate to things outside of your nun's habit and yet remain true to what it symbolized that captured my attention and won my admiration.

My memories of conversations with you are linked with the beginning of my real questions about the world I was in and the worlds I had yet to encounter.

You never dwelt on the predictable or the obvious, which was a great relief in a learning environment that was premised on the idea of the teacher as the expert and the student as the passive recipient of knowledge and direction. I remember your English classes as an invitation to think and a place where

14

unorthodox ideas could be broached even if they didn't fit in the predictable scheme of things. Yes, we still sat in rows and rose politely to answer or ask questions, but somehow, despite the constraints that these rituals imposed, you set the scene for your students to genuinely reflect on important ideas.

I remember the stark contrast of coming into your classroom after leaving my French class where the sole objective most of us had was to endure forty minutes of drill without exposing ourselves to humiliation through a pronunciation or grammatical error that our French teacher seemed to take as a personal affront. In the five minutes that passed between leaving that classroom and entering yours, I often felt a sense of relief and anticipation...relief that I was out of the danger zone for another day, and anticipation that something interesting might happen, or something I hadn't thought about before might be raised and the forty minutes would pass quickly.

Years later, when I was an educator myself and, subsequently, as Director of Education for the Toronto Board of Education, I spent a lot of time thinking about how to create the context and the climate for transformational learning. I often remembered the characteristics that made your classroom a place I wanted to be. An American educator, Carol Ann Tomlinson, speaks about the things that make learning "irresistible." I now think she must have channelled your classroom or classrooms like it when she identified the feelings that truly excellent teaching evokes. Tomlinson speaks of creating a sense of affirmation, contribution, purpose, power, and challenge. As I recall my experiences in your Grade 11 English class, and my many discussions with you outside of the classroom, I think that what you offered resulted in my experiencing all of those reinforcing and encouraging messages. I did indeed feel affirmed as a legitimate inquirer whose perspective was worthy of respect. You created an atmosphere where kids felt they had a contribution to make, even if it was off the beaten path.

Perhaps that was because we knew that we weren't following a formula or a prearranged agenda in the discussions you led or helped us carry. There was always a sense of shared purpose and a spirit of reciprocity in creating the learning agenda. I always felt that I had some power to help shape what we paid attention to and to even, on occasion, change the course of our explorations if something pressing or captivating emerged.

I think the idea of challenge was also very prominent in your classroom. While I remember feeling like an invested participant who gave and took away good things from the class most days, I also remember feeling pushed to think harder or longer about ideas that were new or foreign to me. And if you think about the meaning of the Latin homonym for education, *educo,* "to lead out," "lead forth," "take out," or "raise up," that is about the best thing that could happen in a learning situation.

Many years after I left high school, and long after our paths had ceased to cross, I found myself in a very unusual situation. I was the Director of Education for the Toronto Board of Education and you were retiring as a Principal from the Toronto Catholic School Board. Purely by luck, I was at a meeting where some of the organizers of the event celebrating your many years of contribution as an educator were talking about finding former students to speak in your honour. There was my opportunity to say thank you in a very public way for the profound impact you had on me as an emerging adult. It was the invitation to inquiry and the confirming support that you provided, which contributed to my sense that I could assume leadership roles and, in some ways, serve as a catalyst for the growth of others, first in my own teaching practice and later in the leadership roles I would assume. Ironically, the openness and expansiveness of the dialogues that you fostered with your students led me to venture outside the protected ethos created by the convent school where we first met to ultimately make my mark in the public education system. You helped equip me to make choices and to take risks. I was so happy to be able to say that to a large audience of your admirers and colleagues—some of whom may have wondered why I had "strayed" from the Catholic tradition which educated me to become part of the secular system. Ironically, the gifts you gave me are exactly what enabled me to see myself in roles outside of my initial comfort zone.

"Greatness in teaching is just as rare as greatness in medicine, dance, law, or any other profession. Although the qualities that make great teachers are not easy to inculcate or duplicate, watching a great teacher at the top of his or her form is like watching a great surgical or artistic performance. Although infinitely difficult and painstakingly planned, great teaching appears effortless and seamless. One can easily believe that it is the simplest thing in the world—until one tries to do it"(Mark Goldberg, *The Qualities of Great Teachers*, Chapter 26). I did watch you do it and I learned in my own classroom how tough and complex an act you were to follow. I will be forever grateful that I had a front row seat in your audience when I was sixteen, and the world (and my place in it) was still to be discovered.

With affection, respect, and fond memories,

Joan Green.

A Letter to the Teacher I'll Never Forget

by
Marcia Johnson

Dear Ma'am,

I have been given the challenge of writing a letter to the teacher I'll never forget. That teacher is you. Even though I don't remember your name, I'll never forget you.

I wonder if you remember me. I was really thin, had large eyes, big teeth, and my hair was in about ten braids tied with ribbon. That last descriptor probably describes most of my female classmates in Old Habour Bay, St. Thomas, Jamaica, in the mid-sixties. I don't remember. But, like I said, I definitely remember you.

When I was reunited with my parents in Canada after having been apart from them for three years, I told them what my days were like with you. They didn't believe me. According to them, it was all in my wild imagination, and they laughed at my ridiculous stories. Now I understand the laughter. No parent wants to believe that harm would come to their child at the hands of someone they trusted. I see that now, but, in the moment, I felt horribly betrayed.

I remember your small house next to the school. As you know, the school was really just a shelter. My fellow students and I sat on benches and used slates and chalk to do our work. Every morning, you would take a wooden plank, reach over, and slam it onto one of the supports to create a ramp from your stoop to the school. This was our cue to stand. I would watch out of the corner of my eye as you dragged your one-legged, three

18

hundred pound self over to start your day with us. We stood quietly as you hopped laboriously to the front of the class using various shoulders or heads to steady yourself. Then, you perched on a stool. For the rest of the day, we were subjected to your tyranny. I, personally, vowed every day to be the best student, the best girl, the best human in the world. If those achievements weren't possible, I prayed to be the first person ever to perfect the art of invisibility.

As I got older, I reclaimed the experience. I turned it into a joke. This is how I told it on stage, January 26, 2001:

"After she'd finished hopping to the front of the class, she'd sit on a stool where she stayed for the rest of the day. You might find this hard to believe, but she was an extremely bitter person. We would get the strap for just...being there! But, since she was on the stool, we had to walk all the way to the front of the class to get the punishment. And at the end of every day, she would pick one of the girls to stay behind and help her cook dinner. On the days that she chose me, I would pray with all my heart that I wouldn't make any mistakes. Imagine being four- or five-years-old and chopping onions or peeling potatoes. If I didn't get it just the way she liked, she'd smack me on the head. To this day, I can't cook Jamaican food."

You'll be proud to know that this story got several laughs throughout and a big laugh at my lament over not being able to cook food from my birth country. People thought that I'd exaggerated for effect. "No one could really treat young children that way."

Do you feel any guilt?
Upon reading the story straight, without performing, without pretending to cry at the end, without waiting for the audience's reaction, it reads like the testimony of a child abuse victim. In fact, if you were to exhibit the same behaviour today in Canada, you would be charged with that crime and be

sentenced to prison. Prison! Because, Ma'am, it *is* child abuse. Plain and simple.

I so wanted to write a positive letter, a letter about a teacher who gave me wings, who made me believe in myself. Well, I wouldn't be able to narrow down the list to just one teacher, not because they were all so brilliant, but because, in comparison to you, even my worst Canadian teachers were kind, patient, and encouraging.

I have somehow fallen into teaching. I understand now the frustrations of trying to keep a class of thirty plus people focused, of getting them to retain basic information. Sometimes, I have had those flashes of anger. My memories of your classroom are part of what help me to quell it. I couldn't imagine laying hands on a student, even though they are adults and would be in a better position to defend themselves than I was. Hitting a student would be a sign of my failures as a teacher. I don't want to be like you.

About five years after I'd arrived in Canada, a family friend visiting from Jamaica mentioned you to my parents. He referred to you as that "miserable, one-footed teacher." I remember my mother saying: "Oh, that's the woman Marcia told us about." I was vindicated! But, instead of apologizing for doubting me, my parents laughed about it. I'd gotten used to living with them again, so I understood the laughter. There was no time to fret about things in the past. We were living in a new country and living with new people and new customs. Why waste energy on a miserable, one-legged woman hundreds of miles away? They had a point.

I finally have compassion for you. I'm guessing that you lost your leg to diabetes. That's a horrible thing to go through.

No one treats people the way you treated us unless they have been on the receiving end of the same or worse kind of abuse. You shouldn't have taken it out on us.

I hope that things turned out well for you. They certainly did for me.

Sincerely,

Marcia Johnson.

A Letter to the Teacher I'll Never Forget

by
Carolyn Peters

Within the span of my 69 years, I've had dozens of teachers: ballet teachers, piano teachers, art teachers, swimming teachers and many, many more too numerous to mention here. But when I hear the word "teacher," I automatically think "school," and think about "The Teachers I'll Never Forget."

All of the neighbourhood kids started school a whole year before me. That fall, winter, and spring was long and lonely, with only my grandmother and aunt as companions. So you can imagine how my excitement mounted, as, week by week and day by day, the summer of '47 ended, and September began.

My mother actually never said to me, "You're starting school today." But one morning, the household routine seemed to stray from the usual, and I knew something was up. My grandmother was in the kitchen, ironing my new pink dress with the eyelet trim, and Auntie Idy was on the back porch, polishing my white party shoes. My mother and I were upstairs, in our bedroom, where she was performing "The Ritual of the Hair Ribbons," a special ceremony reserved for birthdays and holidays. After I was dressed, I was thoroughly inspected, from head to toe, by all three women. Then my mother picked up her purse and slipped into her white gloves, so I knew it was time to leave. But where were we going? When we reached the corner of our street, we turned left, instead of right to the streetcar stop. Now, I knew...this was the day...this was the day I was going to school!

I could hardly contain my excitement as I skipped up the stairs and through the front door of the old brick building. I quickly let go of my mother's hand and started running. But just as I turned the corner to the classroom hallway, I froze on the spot. Stretching, as far as I could see was a writhing rabble of wailing children; billions and trillions of crying children, and I joined in the chorus right along with them.

Tightly gripping my mother's hand, I reluctantly inched forward with the crowd. As I neared the end of the line, exhausted and bleary-eyed, I could see a tall man in a white jacket. And I could see each panic-stricken child, with sleeves rolled up and tears rolling down, desperately trying to escape his grasp, only to be caught by the arm and stabbed!

After that traumatic first day, I have very few recollections of school, or teachers, until grade three. My grade 3 teacher was Mr. Johnson. Was Mr. Johnson an outstanding teacher? Honestly, I don't remember. But what I do remember is what happened in his classroom one morning, just before recess. Mr. Johnson, standing at the front of the class, took a small photo from the right-hand pocket of his suit jacket. It was one of those old black-and-white photos with perforations around the edges, as if my budgie had been nibbling at it. He told us the photo had come all the way from Africa. A quiet titter arose when Mr. Johnson handed the photo to Tommy Berris; row one, seat one. With our collective eyes fixed on Tommy, the quiet twitter rose to a din as we witnessed his face suddenly freeze. Tommy looked like he had been stunned by Flash Gordon's ray gun. After what seemed like forever, Tommy carefully passed the photo back to Susie; row one, seat two. Suddenly, Susie started crying and threw the source of her discontent back to the next kid.

My anxiety and anticipation rose to a feverish pitch as that photo was passed, from one hand to another, leaving each classmate with either a look of awe or of horror on their faces. Miraculously, the photo materialized in my hand. And, in only a flash of time, the image of that photo was burned into my brain for all eternity. It was snake: a very large, very long, very scary SNAKE, with its belly slit open, from head to tail! My eight-year-old brain, which as of yet did not have the experience of television, could not fathom why a baby deer was sleeping on the grass, beside the dead snake.

OH! MY! G-D! It was the snake's "Last Supper!"

Following closely upon this life-altering experience, came Miss Knechtal, who is the teacher responsible for my standing before you here today. Miss Knechtal wanted to encourage my talent for writing by keeping me after school, once or twice a week. Did you know that 100 lines of "*I will not talk in class*" filled three sheets of foolscap? During the remainder of my time in primary school, I continued to practice my writing, and consumed one thousand, four hundred, and eighty-six more pages.

There are also many high school teachers that I'll Never Forget. Miss O'Brien is definitely on my list. She taught English and Art; I managed only a C+ in both classes. The problem, as I saw it, was that I was totally distracted by Miss O'Brien as a "fashionista." On the day she returned from Christmas vacation, she swung into the room, and, with platinum hair flying, showed off her new vest which, I'm sure, had once been a carpet on the floor of a Mexican hacienda. Moreover, Miss O'Brien tried to coordinate her glasses with her new outfit by painting the frames with "Hot Tamale Red" nail polish.

You would never have guessed that Mr. Peebles, who sported wire-rimmed glasses and a bowtie, would be the only Latin teacher that could make a dead language come alive. There was no other classroom filled with so much laughter, and there was no other classroom where the walls reverberated with the singing of "Rudolph the Red-Nosed Reindeer" in Latin!

Mr. Peebles was the only one of my teachers who truly understood the significance of a high school education. "You are not here to learn math, or science, or even Latin; you are here to learn how to think. The only Latin lesson you will remember, 10, 20, or even 50 years from now, is tu, tui, tibi, te, tu, te." Well, as you can see, Mr. Peebles was absolutely right!

As with all firsts, the first day of high school was a significant and momentous event. At 9:00am on Tuesday, September 3rd, 1957, I anxiously sat, with 34 other grade-niners, awaiting the arrival of our homeroom teacher. Just as the bell rang, she boldly strode through the door, and, following tradition, wrote "Mademoiselle Will" on the blackboard. Carefully, replacing the chalk on the blackboard ledge, she turned to speak:

"This is the last time you will hear English spoken in this class."

...dead silence...

Then, Mademoiselle Will casually walked over to Roz, row 5, seat 1, and extended her right hand. With a clear voice, she introduced herself: "Je m'appelle Mademoiselle Will." Roz, hesitantly raising her right hand and barely touching Mademoiselle's, stammered, "Jam pell Roz...". "Bon"! said Mademoiselle Will, as she continued down the aisle, to the next desk, and to Roz's relief. When she arrived at my assigned seat, I struggled to my feet, and, shyly shaking her hand, I squeaked out, "Je m'appelle Carolyn." "Bon!" said Mademoiselle Will, and continued down the aisle.

This was our very first class of the very first day of high school, and we learned enough French to ask the one question we needed most: "Puis-je aller aux toilettes?"

Dear Miss Will,

I always remember you perched on the edge of your desk, wearing a classic but stylish dress. You wore no earrings, no brooches, no bracelets; just a watch with a black leather strap. Your dark hair was held in place by a simple pin, and you wore no makeup, except for a thin swipe of red lipstick. You are "Simply Elegant!"

You inspired us with your tales of your travels abroad, and you intrigued us with the stories of the French authors: Balzac, Dumas, Flaubert...

Mademoiselle Will, I think you would be pleased to know that you even motivated me to read *Madame Bovary* and *Les Misérables* on my own time. Every night, I lay awake reciting my French homework, just in case you called upon me to translate. I worried that I wouldn't be able to give you a "perfect performance." I worried that I, Carolyn Peters, *your* student, would disappoint you or let you down. To lose your respect was my worst fear of all.

For the first forty minutes of our day, you were an actress, striding across your stage, stabbing the air, waving your arms, frowning, laughing, crying, doing just about anything to communicate the lesson. Your passion was inexhaustible. And, without our realizing it, we were learning a new language as your passion – for French and for life – transferred to us.

Although my facility in French has greatly diminished over the years, there are other lessons, your Life Lessons, which have endured and guided my thoughts and actions since those early days. Not only were you a great French teacher, but you were also a great raconteur, a philosopher, a motivational speaker, a coach, and a mentor. You were the person who gave me the tools I needed for living an exceptional life.

SEASON 3: PART TWO

A LETTER TO MY HOMETOWN
January 19, 2014

Shirley Barrie

Jen Cook

Jo Lampert

Diana Tso

A Letter to My Hometown

by
Shirley Barrie

Dear hometown,

I could hardly wait to leave you. If it hadn't been for my family, I would never have gone back. *Good riddance, shake the dust,* thought my arrogant young self.

But looking back, I can acknowledge that, while being a teenager was often agonizing, being a child was bliss.

We lived at the corner of North Broadway and Venison St. East. Venison St. East was a little stub that dead-ended at a gulley. Broadway – and to this day it still *is* a Broad Way – ran through the centre of town. North Broadway was residential. My father was an interloper, having opened a business - the G.A. Barrie Funeral Home - in the big corner house. We lived upstairs.

When I was small, my "friends" were the old people who lived around us. Miss Maddox was an elderly socialite and former owner of the stationery store. She would occasionally invite me in for tea, served in delicate china cups in her figurine-filled living room. The Turners, who lived behind us in the house beside the gulley, thought their kids should quit school after Grade 8, and the "truant officer" was a regular visitor. But Mr. and Mrs. Turner would invite me into their dark, gloomy kitchen. I was terrified, but the lure was extra old cheddar cheese and crackers, which I loved. On the other side of us lived Mr. and Mrs. Hiya. Their name was actually Grass, but "hiya!" was how they always greeted me. I'd watch Mrs. Hiya bake bread in the morning, and Mr. Hiya eat his lunch of poached egg on a bed of boiled spinach. I couldn't imagine eating spinach, let alone doing it every day, and it fascinated me. In the afternoons, after Mr. Hiya had gone back to work, I'd sit outside the house, watching the window of Mrs. Hiya's bedroom, waiting for the blind to go up—the sign that her rest was over and I could visit.

Then one day, I saw a little girl in the front yard of the big house on the other side of Broadway. We stood on the boulevards and looked at each other—for days. Finally, I begged my mother to take me across to play. Sonja and her parents had moved in to her grandmother's Nursing Home to "help." We had to run a gauntlet of old people desperate for company but there was great fun to be had at the "home," including making an un-flushable "soup" in the toilet from supplies we found in a usually locked cupboard.

In the basement of the nursing home were bushel baskets of old clothes. We'd deck ourselves out in long dresses, high heels, hats, gloves, purses and jewelry, then clomp our way up and down the street. One day I persuaded Sonja to follow me across Broadway in our finery. We clomped our way up the front walk of the funeral home and rang the doorbell. When my Dad opened the door, I said, "We're here for the visitation."

We only did that once.

Sonja moved to the other side of town, and I discovered the aforementioned gullies. In Toronto, they'd be called ravines. I was in High School before people in my hometown discovered that there were advantages to houses backing onto "ravines." Before that, they were just waste spaces that you had to circumvent. I made friends with Barbara, who lived on one of the Concessions. In summer, I'd leave in the morning taking a package of hotdogs, or buns – we'd share around - and we'd spend the day adventuring in the gullies: plowing through woods, wading through streams, building bridges, catching frogs and cooking them in old tin cans. As long as I was home in time for supper, nobody seemed bothered.

But what about the gulley right at the stub end of Venison St.? It was guarded by the old troll who lived beside it, and she'd come out and yell at us if we got within six feet of the edge. She phoned our parents, threatening that "she'd have a heart attack if those kids didn't stay away from the gulley." But as we got older, we got bolder. We ignored the troll. (Or she got too ill to be such a bother). Instead of hanging around at the top, we'd plunge down the precarious slope to the wonders that awaited us.

It was ours...except in August. We were forbidden to go anywhere near the gulley then, because it could be dangerous. We were never sure what "dangerous" meant, but it had something to do with tobacco harvest. Yes, my hometown was in the heart of tobacco country. In fact, hometown, you were later immortalized by Stomping Tom Connors: *My back still aches when I hear that word. Tillsonburg.* The migrant workers came largely from Quebec. The town provided no services, and those who didn't find work bedded down in the gullies and begged door-to-door for food.

It took a long time for the town to get more actively involved; a long time to end the Black and White Minstrel Shows that the Rotary Club put on every year, or to erase the by-law that forbade a black from staying overnight in town.

Although my political consciousness was still pretty unformed, you seemed to grow smaller as I grew bigger. Everybody knew everybody, and tales were told. My then boyfriend was the son of the minister of our church. He thought he was respecting his dad by going to another town to drink with his buddies during a hockey game. But someone saw, of course, told my Dad, and I was forbidden to see him. Like *that* had the desired effect. Boyfriend became husband—and still is! My aunt and grandparents had a constant mantra for my sisters and me

31

as we grew up. "Barrie girls don't do that," "Barrie girls don't go there," "don't wear that," "don't say that," "don't..."

To my hyper-religious family, smoking was also a sin, but in a twist of logic that defied my youthful understanding, they were perfectly happy that I work in harvest every year. I've never been an early riser, so my Mom would wake me up, make my breakfast, and literally push me out the door for my 6:30 am ride to the farm. I hated the work, but hey, it was money for university, and boy did I want to leave.

My Dad died, my Mom re-married, my stepfather died, but my mother stayed. And over the years, I gradually learned the up-sides of a now not-so-small town, but still a caring community. As my mother's vision faded, her determination didn't. Several times a week, she walked up town with her white cane. I asked her once, how she managed to cross Broadway to her bank. "Oh, I just stand on the corner," she said, "and pray that someone will come and help me across. And someone always does."

Last year I went back to the – gasp – 50th reunion of my High School graduating class. I re-connected with Sonja, who never left. I learned that one of my best friends from High School had just moved back, as had several other classmates. I won't be joining them, but I will look to support ways that a big city, too, can "help people across."

A Letter to My Hometown

by
Jen Cook

To my hometown, Geraldton,

As I begin writing this letter, I realize that whenever someone asks where I grew up, I only ever say: "just a little mining town in Northern Ontario." I never bother to say your actual name; I always assume that no one knows who you are. Like most assumptions, it's not entirely true. It turns out there are people who know you and – more surprising to me – they like you.

In many ways, you offered me a pretty idyllic childhood. I grew up on a lake outside of town. My dad had a Cessna 180 float plane that he docked five minutes from our house. Most summer mornings, my sister and I, and eventually our brother, would take turns getting up at 5:30 in the morning to go down to the plane, so we could fly into our favorite fishing spot about a half-hour away. My dad would land the plane on a sand bank, in a little cove. We'd fish from the floats and catch our limit of pickerel every time. I'm guessing that's where my love of early mornings came from. Watching the sun rising over the stillness of the water, the air a bit cool without the heat of the sun, just my dad and me. On many of those flights, we watched herds of caribou, moose, or wolves running beneath us, my dad getting as low as he could so we could get a good look. I had no idea then, how remarkable that was! In the winter, when it was 30 below, we'd snowshoe through the trees surrounding our house, and spend several hours a day skidooing, ice fishing, and skating on the lake. I think I spent more time outside than inside growing up.

And we were safe...well, except for frostbite and falling through the ice. But other than that, we never had to worry. What a gift!

My parents had grown up in Southern Ontario. They married at 19- and 21-years-old, and made the move to Northern Ontario for work. It was my dad's dream to live off the land *and* get away from his parents, and you provided the perfect spot. We always had a huge vegetable garden, and my dad hunted moose and deer every year. That, plus the fish we caught made up the majority of what we ate through the winter. Until I moved to the city, I didn't even know people bought fish. A portion of my summer vacation was always spent chopping and piling wood that we would then use to heat our house throughout the winter. My dad loved it—it was everything he had wanted.

As for me, yes, of course I loved all the things we had and could do, but I quietly felt like there was always something more important to my dad than me, and it wasn't just my siblings. I couldn't put my finger on it, but it just wasn't right. As the first-born, I thought I had earned "first right of refusal," but for some reason I kept coming second to something I didn't yet have words for. Turns out my dad was a "drinker." The word I was looking for (but no one ever said while I was growing up) was "alcoholic." Most of my teens were spent fighting with my dad. I can't recall what the fights were about, only that they started out innocent enough and then would spiral uncontrollably into an illogical screaming match that would eventually end with: "if you don't like it, leave." I always did, feeling both hopeless and furious at the same time, with no other option but to come back once I calmed down.

By the time I left home at 17, the feelings I had for you, my little mining town, were completely obliterated by my anger towards my father, and the feeling that all of this was my fault. I just wasn't good enough. That's what living in a small town had come to represent to me. Not a place of adventures, dreams and comfort, but a place where there were no choices, where it was okay to drink too much, yell at people, never apologize—a place where my feelings didn't matter. Hearts were being torn repeatedly, and it seemed like nobody could do anything about it. Once I graduated, I left for good and swore I'd never go back!

In 2004, after an extremely busy and stressful five years, my husband and I sold our house in the city and bought 200 acres north of Bancroft at the end of Scott Line Road. The property had four cabins, a barn, and a lake that was surrounded by crown land. It was ripe with possibility. We were exhausted and wanted to see what it was like to live life a little more simply. Our plan was to renovate the cabins and live there...with no running water or electricity, I might add. Crazy, yes, but so exciting! That first summer, we were blessed with gorgeous weather and our days were spent working outside all day, ripping things apart, getting the tractor running, cutting the grass, chopping wood and piling it for the winter, only taking breaks for a swim to cool off and for lunch and dinner, which we cooked on the barbecue. If I could stay awake long enough, we'd watch the sun go down. I was in the best shape of my life. We were off the grid, tearing things down and building them back up with our own two hands and having a blast.

As with all things, it wasn't only sunshine and lollipops, and as two very strong, independent people with big ideas, we had our fair share of heated arguments. It was mid- afternoon, the sun was shining, we were hot and dirty and things weren't going particularly well when the argument started. As it gained momentum, I heard myself beginning to yell, and as I got more frustrated, the yell started to turn into a scream and then I heard this voice loud and clear in my head say: "this is your childhood all over again." I stopped dead in my tracks. Oh, my God! Is that what I've done? Is this what I'm doing? Recreating my childhood? Am I destined to replay my parents' life no matter how hard I try to avoid it? At that point it had been years since my dad had stopped drinking, yet here I was, still replaying that old story.

It's been my experience that, unfortunately, you can't create the future without looking at the past. As I looked around from this vantage point, surrounded by people I loved and was proud of, I could see clearly that it hadn't been where I had grown up that I had run away from at 17—I ran from my dad, his drinking, and the feelings that went along with that. So it wasn't the past I was recreating; it was my future that I was creating with things I loved from my past. Sadly, the process isn't foolproof, and old stories die hard. However painful, I knew I had to weed through the past in order to fully live my own story, my way.

It has taken some time, but I have come to realize that you, Geraldton, had been part of my saving grace in all the chaos of my teens. I ran to you when I walked out of the house after fights with my dad. It was you who offered comfort and space for my feelings, always without judgment. You kept me safe. And you contributed to my belief that anything is possible.

After so many years of blaming you and feeling ashamed that I came from "just a little mining town in Northern Ontario," it feels so much better to be able to proudly say: "I'm from Geraldton, Ontario. It's an amazing place." I'm sorry it took me so long to say this, but, thank you. Thank you from the bottom of my heart for giving me the space and opportunity to explore, have adventures, believe in simple things, to dream and, of course, to fight. Because without some fight, you can't realize your dreams.

With love and gratitude,

Jen Cook

A Letter to My Hometown

by
Jo Lampert

Dear Toronto,

I came "home" for a visit on December 31st, just in time this year for the "polar vortex." I'm told that Canada was colder this year than Mars, which makes me sentimental, and gives me a warm, glow-y Canadian feeling. Exiting the airport, I recognised the smell at once: doughnuts and ice. My kids couldn't smell it, but me, I knew that smell. Doughnuts and ice.

I'm from these frozen loins. I've been away twenty years, but this is my landscape, and my city.

Now I live in Australia. I love my family and friends in Brisbane, but I am not from those hot loins. When it was -22 degrees in Toronto last week, it was plus 45 in Brisbane. While I was re-learning how to walk on sheets of treacherous ice, 24 hours away my husband and everyday friends were lying under ceiling fans, looking for the closest neighbour with a pool, a gin, and a tonic. I don't think people know how much of us is made of weather.

An immigrant's life is a fragmented life with a before and an after. "That happened when I was a Canadian, this happened in Australia." "I used to do things that way, but now I do things this way." There will come a time, not quite yet but not so far in the future, when I – astonishingly – will have spent as much of my life there as here, but somehow Canada will always be home. Canada owns me – it's where my mother is, and it's the land that raised me.

I was just a little girl living in Toronto when Expo '67 presented Ontario with the best theme song, ever. We belted out the lyrics in classrooms in Ontario that whole year long. It was remarkably satisfying to sing it out in unison. *Ontari-ari-ario. A Place to stand, a place to grow.* Hokey or not, the tune brought tears to our eyes (or at least this is how I remember it).

I grew up in a privileged part of the city, on Heathdale Road near Bathurst and St Clair. At the end of our street was Cedarvale Ravine, complete with squirrels, chipmunks, skunks, cardinals, blue jays and robins. As kids, we spent many days over at that ravine, riding double on our bikes down the hill. Heathdale Road was on the edge of multicultural Canada – at that time Italian, Greek, West Indian, and Jewish. In my youth, I was completely, utterly urban. I recall the excitement when the new Spadina subway line was built, making it even easier to go downtown. I spent my teenage years hanging around the Smokestack at Vaughan Road Collegiate, hanging out in discos, loitering in The Eaton Centre.

I became an adult in Toronto, too. Toronto was both a place of culture and politics. I took it for granted that everyone knew their country's poets, paid what they could for plays on Tuesday nights, and protested at City Hall when something in *Now! Magazine* ignited the fire in their belly.

But then...

One day in 1990, I was sitting in the staffroom of Seneca College where I taught English. I had just finished a Masters at OISE. I was a bit bored, newly single, and a bit restless, when I picked up a binder from the staffroom table. Turns out it was from an Australian looking for a Toronto teacher to exchange with (he'd met a Canadian girl backpacking and, well...you know). That night I phoned him, and by the next day the deal was done. I was young and I gave it little thought. It sounded like an adventure, so off I went to Cairns in North Queensland, Australia. Here's what I previously knew about Australia: Crocodile Dundee, kangaroos, Sydney opera house, *My Brilliant Career*, Olivia Newton-John, and...nope. That's about it.

I flew out of YYZ on December 31st (-25 degrees C) and walked out onto the airport tarmac in Cairns on January 2nd (+35

38

degrees C). Much like this year, in reverse. When I walked onto the tarmac that year, I couldn't yet identify the smell. I thought it was vaguely skunk, but learned later it was rainforest mulch.

And here are some of the things I learned that year: a truckload of Australian slang, how to camp (turns out this is quite different from how to ride a subway), how to shear a sheep (well maybe not, but I watched a woman shear a sheep in Goondawindi), and all about Aboriginal dispossession (something that shamefully had been invisible to me in Toronto, though its repercussions in Canada paralleled what I learned in Australia). I laughed at place names like Goondawindi and Burpengary (where my mother-in-law lives), but my husband laughs just as much at Nippising. Ni-*piss*-ing, he says, pissing himself laughing.

And I fell in love, doing exactly as my mother warned me not to. I met an Australian, married him, shuffled back and forth for a few years while we had children and dithered about, and then ended up – much to my astonishment – permanently living in Brisbane, Australia (though lucky enough to return, regularly, to T.O). Now, it's been more than twenty years (which cannot be the case, but somehow is).

When I am in Brisbane, I call Canada "home"; when I am in Toronto, I feel Australian. My weird hybrid accent now sometimes gets mistaken for Irish, though I haven't an Irish bone in my Jewish-Canadian body. I get stupidly excited when I am in Toronto by inane things like shopping in Loblaws, purchasing bus tokens, ordering my coffee double double (instead of getting a "flat white"), and ordering pop (I don't even like it, I just like saying it). Moving from an English-speaking country to an English-speaking country (sort of) is a strange, surreal kind of immigration. Humour took me a long time to understand, but the myths are true. Canadians are gentler and more polite, while Australians (that's me now, some of the time) are sharper-edged and their humour is more teasing.

I stopped being offended quite so easily when I moved to Australia. I also stopped feeling like I had to share all my feelings. In Australia, that's not so much a sign of emotional health as proof of emotional wankiness. Shut up and get on with it. It's an adjustment, and still, when I'm "home" (and I mean Toronto now), there's a bit of me that feels more "true" – not very postmodern of me, but it's the way it is. Still, sometimes now I'm this, and sometimes now I'm that. Sometimes I sit in cafes drinking martinis (that's Toronto) and sometimes I camp, drinking caprioscas on the beach (well, turns out that's not so different after all, is it?. I live an odd life of constant comparisons. Recently, a friend from working-class Australia explained "goon sac" to me. A goon sac is a carton of cheap rotgot wine – the kind that comes in a cardboard box with a silver bag of red wine inside. Urban Dictionary defines it as, "drunk by youths in Australia due to its low cost, however it promotes vomiting due to its awful taste." The beauty of goon sacs, or so my friend Kelli tells me, is that if you are really drunk, you can play a game of Goon of Fortune, where you string your casks up on a clothes line and try to drink from them. Also, when the cask is finished and you are "maggoted'" (i.e. drunk), you can blow the silver wine bags up into a pillow and pass out on them. Having this cultural knowledge, I can reflect on the Canadian equivalent. In Canada, this is boxed wine, good for hosers who want to get wasted. It's good to find common ground, though frankly, I'm a little too old for goon sacs these days, and, even more frankly, I was brought up with higher expectations. Maybe I'm too "Toronto" to appreciate them fully.

Toronto through and through. I still tear up at "A Place to Grow," and don't start me on Joni Mitchell's *Blue*, or even The Barenaked Ladies. I've been known to sing "Oh, Canada" when pressed, but I can get equally gushy over Australiana as well. If I have a home in Toronto, I also now have a home amongst the gum trees.

So, in conclusion, dear First Hometown, Dear Toronto, thanks for being my first love. Thanks for welcoming me home. Thanks for the thaw.

A Letter to My Hometown

by
Diana Tso

Dearest Paris,

I miss you. It's been 18 years (or nine, if you count my short visit home during the Christmas holidays in 2004). I'm sure you've changed. I have. Do you still have many metro strikes? I used to walk 45 minutes to school when the workers decided not to drive your underground trains. Is the public more aware of terrorist bomb threats today? I remember the city sealing all the green igloo bins that recycled glass bottles. We didn't know then that it was the threat of terrorism. You felt safer than Toronto and more creatively dangerous, because I could cross the line and remain anonymous. You made me at once vulnerable and daring in my search for my voice as an artist, as a person, as a woman. You were the hometown that seduced me and pushed me into that space of freedom.

I realized my journey here brought to light my diluted Chinese ancestry and my Canadian uncertainty and safety. The school secretary was surprised to find out that I was "pure" Chinese, meaning to her that both my birth parents were Chinese. I was identified as Canadian, and for some strange reason they thought that I was "mixed": part Chinese and something else. Someone inquired at the school, looking for a "pure" Chinese actress for a film shooting in Rome. She got me an audition and said that if I got the part, the few days I'd miss of school would pay for the rest of my year's tuition. I went to the audition, confused but hopeful, yearning for this lottery moment to fund my expensive theatre school tuition. I returned home opening the Chinese New Year gifts my mom had mailed me, which arrived at the school and brought to light the "purity" part of my Chineseness. I never got the part in Rome, but I made it into second year and graduated.

I didn't seem to belong to the Canadian language of "eh," nor the culture of hockey, maple syrup, beavers and moose... Our family said "wah," and "wey." I had no clue about hockey until my first amateur game in the small town of Nelson, British Columbia (on the west coast of Canada) while on tour with a theatre show a year after I left you. Our family never watched hockey. We watched Carol Burnett. My sister and I would belt out the Tarzan call with Ms. Burnett, trying to out "AAAAHH" each other. Do you know about Tarzan or Carol Burnett? Google them.

My friends spoke three to five languages. Lorenzo, from Sicily, raised by a Spanish nanny, schooled in France when it was time to escape army duty... I can't remember how his English was fluent, too. Remember when he bought pastries at your boulangerie café near the Louvre, and how you surprised us in the Latin quarter with a single table awaiting us outside a restaurant: a white tablecloth, wine glasses, silver cutlery. We sat and elegantly devoured our monte-blanche cakes with silver forks! Even though you forgot the wine, you remembered to push away the clouds just enough to warm our faces and highlight our laughter.

But sometimes your nights were scary, like the time Ruth and I had a little Beaujoulais in our blood and voluminous voices tumbling out of our guts into your shadows. We ended up on a street with brick walls on either side. Suddenly, we realized the comforting background buzz of conversations had diminished into dead silence, arresting our footsteps. We saw a group of ten, maybe a dozen men, staring at us and whispering. Somehow, you put a spell on all of us. The men froze like statues. Ruth and I looked at each other, blue and brown eyes making innate decisions. We locked hands, and the six foot Dane and the five foot Chinese-Canadian continued to walk down that street, right past the men, leaving what sounded like eternal silence behind us. Thanks for keeping us safe that night.

Paris, do you remember Nicholas, Anniken, and Anna? I found them all eighteen years later in Sweden. Nicholas and Anniken each fell in love with a Swedish man. Nicholas became a librarian, Anniken opened a nursery, and Anna became a psychiatrist—she has a machine that carbonates tap water! Is your water still undrinkable without boiling it? Remember how Nicholas and I used to talk in southern belle accents while pretending to be cowboys as we made pasta and tossed salads? You'd try to hold back your laugh, peering through the windowpane, making them tremble. You were not vocal with your feelings, but we could sense your passion by the way you moved, directly forward without fear, sharp eyes, with your head tilted sideways – sexy, but no nonsense – and shrouded in the mist of mystery. Each one of them brought little albums of the times we shared together with you. Really beautiful memories!

I remember you ignited my senses on my daily walks from metro Villiers, up rue de Levis's Marché, tasting cheeses, discussing with shopkeepers what I was concocting for dinner while they chose my wine, people's cigarette smoke mingling with freshly baked baguettes and lingering on my clothes and hair like cobwebs. Then up six flights of stairs to my petite chambre de bonne on rue de Saussure, where I shared a Turkish toilette, lit by a candle in a wine bottle for light. My landlord in Toronto was delighted to tell me my neighbors were Chinese. They were caterers and I thanked my lucky stars I could buy Chinese fresh dumplings and pork buns just outside my door and listen to a different dialect of Chinese when I was missing my mom.

Thank you for your stone benches to rest and ruminate on, where Tom and I got high, only once, while dialoguing about our scene in Michel Azama's *La Crusade*. And then, on another Spring afternoon in Rodin's same garden, Orietta and I read aloud Yves Bonnefoy's poetry (I still have his book, marked April

19, 1996, lunch at Passage Brady and Rodin Museum). I sang Nina Simone songs alternating with Orietta's Italian love arias and no one told us to be quiet. Your sunlight found moments to reach out and kiss our cheeks.

From your Place de Clichy district I walked uphill into Montmartre on some weekends. Your path was a boa constrictor of pastry and meat shops, a serpentine twist around every corner, and I'd find myself clutching the black iron gates outside your pink house, the one with the wooden gargoyles who mocked my childlike wonder at the world. I'd write in my journal, sitting slanted on a wrought iron chair, sipping Pastis on ice along one of your 45-degree angled cobblestone roads, overlooking fragments of Montmartre and a broken sunset. I gazed at your beauty, and then my eyes roamed back to the creamy liquor the shape of a ski slope in my glass. Finally, my feet would find a second solace at the steps of Sacré Coeur to hear the faint voices of the choir chopping in and out of the big wooden doors opening and closing, mingled with the happy hollering of children riding white horses on the merry-go-round. You never got dizzy. I learned to love being alone and embracing an inner silence. You made that discovery fantastically and terrifyingly delightful— Thank you!

On my first return to you, four years later, in 2000, a woman across from my old laundry stuck her head out the window, waved, smiled at me and shouted "Bonnes vacances!" as if I were still a student released into summer after eight months of school. I descended into the underground at metro Villiers and was serenaded by a saxophone player busking on the train, playing "Somewhere Over the Rainbow".
I was happy to be home again. I hope to see you soon.

Je t'embrasse,

Fung

P.S. The first thing I do when I move to a new hometown is buy a plant, get a library card and light a candle for dinner. Do you remember?

SEASON 3: PART THREE

A LETTER TO MY FIRST-YEAR SELF
(UNDERGRADUATE EVENT)
February 25, 2014

Kaye Caronongan

Clarrie Feinstein

Sarah Levy

Gillian Scott

Emma Smith

A Letter to My First-Year Self

by
Kaye Caronongan

To my first-year self:

What are you doing in Ottawa? You looked around the campus well ahead of time before making the decision to move there, and even then it gave you that awkward, "let's-get-out-of-here" feeling at the pit of your stomach, didn't it? Why didn't you listen? Although, I'm glad you didn't. There are some amazing people there that you need to meet, and lessons you need to learn before you can move on.

Now, I know that you were fixated by the idea of going to law school and becoming some renowned human rights lawyer, but plans change. People change. *You* will change. It's okay to not know exactly what you want, what you *should* do, and what you *will* do. There's a life beyond your imagined walls that you ought to explore and learn from. Don't get me wrong, making long-term plans is good and it gives you some kind of direction. But the journey, oh the journey—don't look past the importance of your own journey. Life will interject and the plans that you made while aiming at some ideal destination will become obsolete. Your destination might not seem as ideal as you once thought it was. So enjoy the ride, and see where it takes you.

You might be wondering how your plans have changed? Guess. Could it be? You've made mistakes—Gasp! Relax, Chicken Little, the sky isn't falling. Making mistakes is inevitable. In fact, you should be more worried if you weren't making any. How else are you going to learn to pick yourself back up? It seems bad now, but trust me: you'll live. How you react when you make these mistakes is what you should really think about. Accept that the situation happened. and determine how you can move forward.

Meanwhile, I know you think *a lot*. Get out of your head. By all means, you have some incredible thoughts about anything and everything, but that doesn't mean that you should allow yourself to be devoured by your thoughts. Your thoughts are mere constructs of your imagined realities. Don't forget that these are just *imaginings*. The actions you choose to take preceding these thoughts matter far more. Recognize the person everyone else sees in you. You are so much more than you think you are. There's no need to keep on belittling yourself—why would you, anyway? You work hard and you have accomplished so much. Stop beating yourself down! See the beauty in yourself as much as you see it in other people.

Oh, you will meet such beautiful people. They will be there for you despite the repetitive, insecure nonsense you put them through. They, along with God's will, will help you find light at your darkest moments. Boy, did you have some dark days, weeks, even months. Let this period in time be a reminder of the people who stood by you at your weakest point, the ones who continue to be a part of your life regardless of geographic separation. They are your friends. No, they are a part of your family and of yourself. Cherish them, and be grateful of their company. Especially a very special young lady who we will call S.

You met her through your roommate, who you won't necessarily keep in touch with after a while. It was a little awkward at first, but letting yourself open up to S was one of the best decisions you've ever made. She won't tell you what you want to hear, but what you *need* to hear. She will tell you the honest truth, whether you like it or not. Don't question it. Why did you take so long before actually listening to what she was saying? You can be so stubborn sometimes. Do us both a favour and let down your pride. God only knows how much easier things would have been if you didn't cling on to your pride like some kind of safety bar on a roller coaster.

Anyway, *S* went through a lot of excruciatingly painful medical treatments when she was younger but you'll see that those unfortunate instances strengthened her—they didn't break her. She's your sunshine on a cloudy day. When it's cold inside, she'll brighten your day. She's one of your best girls. So don't wait for the most convenient time to visit her when you leave. A seemingly forgotten foe will come back and bring her the same agony. Be there for her as much as she will be there for you. Support her and strengthen her every moment you can. Be *her* sunshine on *her* cloudy days.

What else can I say? What else should you know? I'm sorry I can't give you the answers to your LAWS100C finals, or write your Law & Literature essays. You'll be fine. Don't worry so much about getting the marks you need, because with hard work they will come. Lose yourself in laughter, love and life. Find passion, faith and hope. *You* are my hidden treasure.

Best,

K.

A Letter to My First-Year Self

by
Clarrie Feinstein

Dear *younger* Clarrie,

I am writing to you from the future; not too far into the future, only a year. Nevertheless, a lot has happened in that time span and in retrospect, I could have done first year better, or, should I say, *you* could have done it better, though you haven't really started yet. My goodness this is already getting confusing.

However, I am writing to you, as I wish to be helpful in this tremendous leap you are undertaking in your life. Everyone always stresses the difficulties of university, telling you to prepare yourself for the obstacles and challenges you will face. Of course, you can never fully prepare or know what to expect when endeavoring to tackle the unknown. Now that I have been through this ordeal I will give you the proper advice, which many people tried to offer, but never fully succeeded in telling you...Or should I say, me?

Our immense passion for literature and the arts has led me to turn to no other than the very fine author, Jane Austen. She is, after all, our favourite and most treasured writer. Having read each of her novels numerous times, I am confident in saying that many lessons have been learned from Ms. Austen. I know this might seem unorthodox – you probably expected reassuring words from mom, dad, maybe a professor – but, well, Jane Austen is the most famous of all, so I say she's the safest bet. I will be taking the advice from a book, recently purchased within this year by our father. It is entitled, *Jane Austen's Guide Book to*

Good Manners. There is nothing finer than a manual, especially one set to the spectacular witticisms of Ms. Austen.

Firstly, the chapter, "Manners Makyth Man and Woman," provides a quote from *Sense and Sensibility*: "If I could persuade myself that my manners were perfectly easy and graceful, I should not be shy." Now, here I will say Ms. Austen is wrong. I know I said to take her advice, but on this occasion I will plant my feet firmly on the ground. Be sure of your actions and opinions; do not be so concerned with how you appear to your professors, TAs, or friends. I have taken this to heart in my second year and have embraced the fact that what I might say or do will not always yield the best results. Take risks with your shy and reserved nature, because that is how people grow and learn, which I can already attest to by witnessing my growth throughout this past year.

Secondly, 'The Forms on Introduction," chapter states: "do not be presumptuous in introduction, respect a lady's reputation, and do not attempt to bring friends of different rank together." Unfortunately, if you do this you will have no friends at all. Let us correct Ms. Austen here, for you must always be willing to meet new people and introduce new acquaintances no matter the differences in their characters. Do not be apprehensive when introducing opposites, for you never know where friendships might lead.

Thirdly, "Calling and Conversation." Now here Ms. Austen is accurate in some of her advice. The chapter states, "be sure to leave cards," and "pay, and return calls promptly." In our day and age, this is translated into phone calls, emails, and texting. Never be reserved in being the first one to initiate a conversation with someone on campus or in the classroom. Be free of anxieties when wishing you could have talked to your instructor before handing in a paper. You've always emailed your teachers in prompt fashion, so do not change on that account. Most times these figures can seem superior and are placed on a pedestal, but remember: our mentors are supposed to cultivate our learning. While not all professors and TAs have our best interests at heart, do not be dissuaded in wanting an explanation with an unsatisfactory grade, or an unsubstantiated comment. Always leave your calling card, as you will be heard and noticed. I'm not sure if that is Ms. Austen's advice. It is, however, mine, and that is good enough.

Fourthly, "Dancing and Dining." Here is a chapter that finally shows the exuberance of youth. It states: "Learn to dance—and to dance well," as it will earn you the admiration of admirers, such as in *Mansfield Park* when Mr. Crawford viewed Fanny, "gliding about with quiet, light elegance, and in an admirable time." That may be difficult these days, when dancing is no longer accompanied by a fine waltz, but is now guided by hip-hop and pop music with kids shouting along to the words, (not the definition of elegance). My advice is: enjoy yourself. Confidence from within only strengthens the outside, and joy from the moment is sure to make anyone admire you.

Fifthly, the chapter on "The Subject of Matrimony..." I feel I should stop here. Maybe two hundred years ago, nineteen would have been an eligible age, but now it's not even contemplated.

I'm afraid the advice of Ms. Austen has not proven to be most beneficial. I thought that with her wit and expertise she would provide the best knowledge and wisdom of all on how to succeed in first year. However, no one can truly offer advice that will make first year easier. If I were to go back to your position now and witness how far I have come along, I believe only a certain sense of pride would erupt. I'm not saying I am completely formed. I am still in the process of finding and maturing myself, but I notice the subtle nuances. Writing and conceptualizing essays is slowly becoming easier, and joining all of the wonderful extracurricular activities at UofT this year has completely changed my feelings towards this vast campus, as I am now experiencing a community I never felt before. These changes are only positive and hopefully my progress will increase incrementally with each subsequent year.

This year, I had a frightful moment, when I was not certain that I was in the right field—what can I hope to achieve with a degree in English? Maybe I should have pursued science or math. I cried to our mother, as I had always been so certain that English was my avenue. She comforted me and told me that all people go through this moment; I am not the only one. The next week, I read *Daisy Miller* by Henry James in my American Literature class and I loved that book. The passion for literature was reignited and I knew I was following the right path—at least, for now.

So, my dear, younger self, I leave you with this quote from Ms. Austen because although she might not help in your first year woes and joys, reading her books can save you from the most troubling times and can reaffirm your love of the English language (and why you are paying thousands of dollars to learn it). From my favourite novel, *Pride and Prejudice*, Elizabeth Bennet states, "I declare after all there is no enjoyment like reading! How much sooner one tires of any thing than of a book! -- When I have a house of my own, I shall be miserable if I have not an excellent library." Strive for that library Clarrie, and you will achieve all your desires and aspirations.

From your loving, older self.

A Letter to My First-Year Self

by
Sarah Levy

Dear Sarah,

They say that to know others is smart, but to know yourself is wise. Well, this first year of your university education is going to make you wiser than you ever dreamed—but it's not going to be easy.

As you're reading this, you're waking up after spending the first of many sleepless nights in a new city, a tiny, springy bed, and a room that you're slowly trying to transform from a prison cell into a space to call home. Apart from the nervous excitement that every significant transition holds, you feel entirely ready and at ease. And you are. You've checked all the boxes: you feel academically, socially, and emotionally prepared—but no amount of grounding could have prepared you for what is coming.

Firstly, about yesterday afternoon: Remember when you were sitting in your little frosh group? You definitely noticed the guy sitting across from you—yeah, the one with long, light brown hair, blue eyes, and a leather jacket. You know, the one who invited you to his show after you so unsubtly revealed that you too liked metal during the icebreaker games? Not that you could forget him. Two words about that: tread carefully. More on that later.

Secondly, about the girl who came and knocked on your door at 2 a.m. asking to borrow your sweatpants: she isn't really

56

as crazy as she seems—in fact, she's one of your best friends. When the guy I mentioned, let's call him M, breaks your heart, H will be there. She'll be there to order pizza with you, listen to Fall Out Boy with you, and lie on Philosopher's Walk with you while you stare up at the sky and ponder how you even got there in the first place.

Finally, (I'm not going to sugar coat it), these first few weeks of school are going to turn your life upside down. You're going to have the time of your life living by your own rules, and growing close to your floormates A, C, and H, who will become the most wonderful friends you could possibly ask for. Unfortunately, the start of your year will instead be defined by a profound sense of guilt about leaving home. For leaving your family and your boyfriend, J.

I just can't stress enough how important it is that you leave the guilt behind. You'll spend too many nights wondering if you made the right choice by moving away, not because it wasn't the right decision for you, but because you're worried that it wasn't the right decision for everyone else.

So after you and J spend the next month and a half fighting every single night, you'll come to realise that things ended between you two long before you ever got on the plane. You're holding on because you don't want to prove people back home right. You don't want to be that couple that stereotypically breaks up at Thanksgiving. But these things happen for a reason.

Don't waste your first month of university leaving parties early so that you can fight with him over Skype about how you were five minutes late getting on to Skype. Don't waste your energy feeling guilty because you had the courage and ambition to move away, and he couldn't deal with it. Even though you don't want to give up on your best friend of three years, remember: he gave up on you first, and once he did your relationship was bound to run its course.

Soon after the relatively minor wounds from J heal, you'll enjoy about a month of calm until the storm that is M is going to hit, uprooting life as you know it.

He'll notice your Nietzsche poster on your wall while visiting a friend, and take that as an excuse to ask you out for coffee a few days before the first formal Ball of the year. You'll go, you'll eat, he'll make you fancy tea when you go back to his room, and you'll be starry-eyed. The night of the Ball, he won't go – he's too cool for that sort of thing, of course – but he'll knock softly on your door when the night is done and you'll share your first kiss, and he'll tell you that he felt so happy he could die. And you'll believe it.

So you'll fall hard and all the rest of it, but soon you're going to find out he still hasn't ended it with the other girl from before, for X, Y, and Z reasons. He'll give you a million excuses, and you'll believe them, and when he tells you that he finally ended it with her, you'll believe that too, because he is what you're looking for right now. After a comfortable, drawn-out, (and at times boring), high school relationship, you want to be swept off your feet by a bad boy who you think you can change—but you can't.

You're blinded by the mystery, and drawn in by the allure that this challenge presents. But you should know better. As someone with perhaps too much relationship experience, as the unofficial counsellor of your friend group, you should be able to see right through him.

You should know better than to believe he spent hours writing a unique song "just for you," because when you ask to hear the song again, he'll play you entirely different chords. But you'll hear what you want to hear, and while he strums entirely random strings, you'll trick yourself into feeling singularly special and loved.

So you'll believe him when he tells you that the nail polish left in his room belongs to his sister.

You'll wave down the countless red flags that keep popping up, you'll ignore the warning signs your friends are constantly trying to make you aware of, and you'll justify it all with the misguided Shakespearean notion that "the course of true love never did run smooth."

Right now, there is a battle waging between your head and your heart, and, if you haven't already guessed, your heart will win.

Wanna hear what happens next? You're going to go to away over the Reading Break. You're going to call him. The other girl will answer. When you hear her voice, your head will spin and you'll feel like vomiting, but you won't be entirely surprised.

So even though you're going to go back and triumphantly throw his Batman shirt back in his face, walk across the Quad, and go out with your friends as if nothing even happened, be prepared for the inevitable fall. Now comes the point in the battle between your head and heart when your heart will give out from exhaustion, and your head will reign victorious. Everything you held true about love will turn to ashes in your hands. You'll enter into a pathetic world of drinking, carb-loading, melodramatic music, and *Titanic*. You'll become a cliché.

Sounds pretty bad, right? The thing is, I know that no matter what I write in this letter, no matter how gruesome a picture I paint, you'll ignore it all. Because you're stubborn, and you can't be convinced of anything once your heart is made up. But honestly , even after everything, I don't know if that's such a bad thing. Sure, if you were to heed my warnings you'd be short a heartbreak and a few tear-stained pillows, but what would you learn?

Because eventually you'll realise, after one long summer, that your concept of love cannot be defined by one betrayal, no matter the mark it leaves on you. You're resilient, and eventually you'll find the strength to love again. In time you'll realise that it is more valuable to have your conception of love shattered and restored, than to have never had it shaken at all.

What you'll learn this year is that there is power, not weakness, in falling in and out of love. That, despite what your cynical, shallow generation may say, that putting yourself out there takes strength, and that the ability to be vulnerable with another person makes you daring. That it's better to be able to rinse and repeat, than to let those who are simply not worth it define your happiness. That it's better to be able to look back on all of the highs and lows and surround yourself with memories, because by falling in love and falling apart, you will learn more about yourself than anything else. That, in the end, wounds turn to wisdom.

So when L messages you in the summer telling you to give B a chance, listen to her—it's a risk, sure, but it will be one of the best decisions you'll make. You will enjoy more certainty, passion, and devotion than you've ever known. With him, you'll realise that the head and the heart don't have to be, and shouldn't be, at odds.

Thus, the only advice I'll give you is to not take my advice at all: stumble, fall, and do everything just as you otherwise would.

It's the only way you'll learn that love isn't blindness—it means seeing more clearly than ever before.

A Letter to My First-Year Self

by
Gillian Scott

Dear First-Year Me,

So I got bangs!

I know that you think they won't suit your face or that you won't look good with them, but don't worry... you do.

Assuming you could actually get this letter without tearing a hole in the space-time continuum, my first instinct is to tell you exactly how not to fuck up. Don't get drunk that night in October and regret it. Don't forget you have that Intro to Classics midterm and walk into a room that looks like a scene from the most cliched nightmare ever. I mean, at least you didn't show up naked. Don't take the hurt you feel and magnify it until it takes over everything around you.

Maybe I'd tell you the things you should do instead: choose karaoke over that horrible party during frosh week, and spend a bit more time actually memorizing your German vocabulary.

If I told you all that, if I went step by step and told you everything, maybe I'd be able to spare you from all that went wrong in first year. You shouldn't have to endure it all. Maybe if you changed a couple things here or there it would keep you from tipping over the cliff that you hadn't even seen coming. No heavy thoughts that cover you over like the layer of brown sludge that covers Toronto all winter long. No concerned and awkward glances from people who you don't quite trust enough to confide in. No tense phone calls to the parental units that never happened enough, and yet still happened too often. You could have the first year that you had always imagined while filling out countless applications for schools that you never got to go too.

Here's the thing: you have to make all those mistakes. You're hurting now, but rest assured—we still have trouble remembering what something is like after it's over, and all the shit you end up feeling this year is now a distant memory. The scars have almost disappeared, and for the most part you forget about them. It's not like they were never there, but more like you've grown out of them in the same way you grew out of that blue skirt that you forgot was in the back of your closet; they've faded like the sun-stained polaroids on your wall.

In case you can't tell, you still have that pretentious predisposition towards bad, semi-poetic similes two years from now.

When you look back, it's not those bad times you think about. At least, not too much. It's the nights you spent talking to new friends for hours at a time about anything and everything. It's late dinners and even a stereotypical college party or two. You were brave. You did things that scared you and ended up better for it. You were kind and funny and bright. You learned tough lessons and you made friends that I'm pretty sure will be there for the rest of your life. You even end up being happy. You choose how to remember your past, so fuck everything else and remember the stuff that really matters.

Cards on the table here, first-year me: there isn't any advice that I want to give you, nothing I want to warn you about in advance. To be honest, there really isn't any advice I could give you that would stick. Knowing you (or me), you wouldn't listen to it in the first place. Everything worth knowing is something you have to figure out in your own time. No one, not friends or family or even your future self, can tell you. Fuck up! Make mistakes! Suffer now because it will make your victories taste even sweeter. Even if I told you how to fix every regret, your life would never be exactly as perfect as you want it to be, because that's not the point of life. You just have to live every day as best you can. Experience things with eyes wide open and grab everything you can take with both hands: hurt and happiness, despair and joy, love of all kinds.

Everything that happens is something that will take you

closer to where you need to be.
I love you.
You should love you too.
Maybe one day we'll both get there.

A Letter to My First-Year Self

by
Emma Smith

Howdy partner,

This is your future self. You may be wondering why I addressed you as "partner." No, past Emma, the world has not been taken over by space cowboys. I was having some trouble deciding how to address you. Technically, I am a stranger to you, so normal letter-writing protocol demands formality. However, addressing yourself as "dear" seemed odd, perhaps even vain. Luckily, the last time I went to visit Mom and Dad, I dug up a gem that was quite applicable to my letter-writing predicament. I found a letter written by seven-year-old us; it was a school assignment. Since the world is such a funny place, seven-year-old us was instructed to write to *her* future self. Funnier still, I found this letter not long after getting my Women Writing Letters assignment. How is that for symmetry? As I am tasked with looking back, I am reintroduced to a version of us who was looking forward. According to the laws of symmetry, that means we are both sort of looking at the same thing: you. Seven-year-old us decided to start her letter with "howdy partner"—she was on a *Toy Story* kick at the time—so I decided to do the same.

I guess you are wondering what sort of wisdom I have to share with you. Well, only one year separates us, but it has been a big year. As you read this, you are in your brand new dorm room; it is the first night of frosh week. You are wiping a tear from your eye. You just got off the phone with your best friend, who has just moved in to her new dorm in Waterloo. You are feeling afraid and alone and anxious—a lot of "A" words. I could tell you that this time next year, you will be a frosh leader. I could tell you that you are about to meet the best friends you have ever had. You are going to miss your parents more than you thought you would. Your friend from Waterloo isn't going to be your friend for much longer. I could tell you that you are going to go on some fantastic adventures. You are going to break the rules and get away with it. I could tell you that you need not fear; you are going to manage your course load somehow. I could tell you a lot of things, but we like surprises. I am not here to step on your toes.

So, why am I here? If you are looking for advice, I have picked up some bits and pieces this past year. As much as I would love to warn you that staying up into the early hours of the morning quickly becomes a bad habit, I know that it will not change our night owl tendencies. Besides, most of your best essay writing will happen after the sun has set. It might be a good idea to spend less money. I know, past Emma, Toronto has a fine selection of used records and they are very hard to resist. You could try to eat less pizza, go to the library more, avoid bad haircuts; the list goes on and on. The truth is, you will make a lot of mistakes this year despite any advice that I could give you. You will have many bad moments; at times you will feel stressed, angry, panicked, guilty, ugly, frustrated, helpless, bored, and miserable. However, you will also spend a large portion of your time laughing until your sides hurt, dancing like a giddy fool, and feeling truly touched by the nice things in your life. You will get excited about the things you learn and the people you meet. It is going to be a challenging, and thus, a rewarding, time. The mixture of good and bad experiences is what makes life authentic. So I don't think any advice from me will do you much good. After all, I am here, relatively intact, and I got this way because past me—that's you—did what you did. So, if you just go about your business, you have all of this to look forward to. In all seriousness, it has not been a perfect year for me but it has been a gorgeous one. You are going to be happier than you have ever been. Oops! It seems I am ruining surprises left and right.

I am not sure if this letter will be overly helpful, past Emma. I wish I had some sort of life lesson to neatly tie everything together. You know us; our thought process is like a bee flitting from flower to flower. I guess not much has changed in that regard, seeing as seven-year-old Emma managed to cover everything from her breakfast to unicorns to infinity and beyond in her one-page letter. She has some instructions for us, though. First, she would like us to wear pink, exclusively pink. It seems we have failed her on that score. She also hopes that we have a pony. Unfortunately, we are still pony-less. She wants to make sure that we have learned to fly. Oops. In fact, there is only one request in that letter that we have actually managed to fulfill: "smile lots." It is a simple thing, but that only adds to its charm. We did not fulfill all of seven-year-old Emma's grand plans. I know that I am not quite what you, my first-year self, were envisaging either. Life never turns out quite like what we have in mind. But that does not matter as long as we keep smiling. I think that our smiling faces provide a sense of symmetry, the best kind of symmetry on offer in this imperfect world.

Good luck, past Emma. I hope this made you smile.

As seven-year-old Emma once wrote,

Over and out.

SEASON 3: PART FOUR

A LETTER TO MY 16-YEAR-OLD SELF
April 20, 2014

Gail Benick

Joanne Latimer

Josée Sigouin

Karine Silverwoman

A Letter to My 16-Year-Old Self

by
Gail Benick

It's a clever trick to play on oneself, this task of imagining what you would tell your younger self. Thank you, Tara and Gailey Road, for inviting me to revisit my teenage years, but quite honestly, nothing you might say or do could convince me to go back to being sixteen again. I think this letter to my adolescent self will demonstrate why.

Dear sixteen-year-old Me:

I'm writing to you from Toronto. Got that? Toronto, Canada: the country Americans tend to consider a notional afterthought, if that. You are a dreamy sixteen-year-old, out for stars, as it will be written in your high school yearbook, but even a dreamer like you could not fathom that you would ultimately leave your place of birth and venture beyond the known world of St. Louis, Missouri. Of course, Mom and Dad are begging you to stay home, beseeching you to attend Washington University, which, as they never cease to remind you, is an outstanding school just fifteen minutes from where you live. Obviously, they want to ensure that you remain in close proximity, cocooned safely. But that's not to be.

Trust me. There is life beyond the mahogany dining room table that seats our small extended family, without fail, every Sunday for a four-course meal of chicken soup, brisket, toss salad, and a Jell-o mold with Redi-Whip sprayed on top. If you ever find yourself pining for that table and in need of a tangible reminder of things past, you'll be able to buy one of Mom's Indian Tree dinner plates on Ebay for a good price. Better yet, hide one away now, pack it in bubble wrap and slip it into your knapsack when it's time to start your journey. It may come in handy when you are riding the Greyhound bus to Boston or New York, eating soggy tuna sandwiches that drip mayonnaise onto your lap.

Because you, my dear, are destined to undertake a circuitous route to your final destination, much like Mom and Dad who left their shtetls in Eastern Europe, escaping poverty and the distinct possibility of death, experiencing loss and separation from their parents, the bubbies and zaydies who their grandchildren never knew. That imperative to migrate, to live both here and there, or somewhere in between, is encoded in your DNA. Accept it. And if you ever doubt your ability to adjust to a new environment, to start over as an immigrant, you can be guided by the example of Mom and Dad, who, (let's be honest), had their share of bumps along the way. Yet they never surrendered to the strains created by precarious employment, chronic illness, car crashes, and robberies (just to mention just a few of their experiences that might have cast a shadow over your first decade and a half, but somehow didn't).

So how can you prepare for this journey? I'd like to offer four tips I've gleaned from decades of experience: Given that 68 is the new 43, maybe my advice won't sound quite so antiquated to you.

#1. Embrace the F-word.

And I don't mean the F-word that quite frequently rolls off your tongue. As a sixteen-year-old in the 1960s, you are coming of age just as the second wave of feminism is emerging. Your generation will make significant gains in the struggle for women's rights. You will witness the passage of the Equal Pay Act, the implementation of Title VII of the Civil Rights Act barring employment discrimination based on sex, and the start of affirmative action. Become a feminist. As the acclaimed writer and activist Alice Walker observed, "The most common way people give up their power is by thinking they don't have any." You do have power. Use it. When you are invited to make a presentation to the Rotary Club of St. Louis, welcome the challenge, sit at the table with those male Rotarians, speak your truth and, whatever you do, don't dress up in your best pastel cashmere sweater set with a string of pearls. Just wear black.

#2. Trust your abilities.

Maybe you've already noticed that lots of teenage girls downplay their accomplishments and you, I'm afraid, are one of them. Whenever you take a math test or submit an English essay, you assume you've failed or done miserably. If you do succeed, you claim it was just luck and you fret that you'll never be able to do it again. You walk around feeling like a fraud, or worse: an imposter. Your hair droops over your face, hiding your eyes from view and you constantly shrug your shoulders. Please stop. Adulthood doesn't necessarily come with greater self-confidence unless you work at it. Some women never completely leave the sandbox —or should I say the quagmire — of self-doubt. Your homework, starting this minute, is to resist those negative thoughts you harbor and recognize them for what they are: a form of self-sabotage. Trash that judgmental inner Girl Scout and send her packing.

#3. Get creative.

I know that your high school, University City High, prides itself on creativity in the curriculum, providing oodles of opportunities to excel in music, literature, drama, and the visual arts. And of course, we can't possibly forget that Tennessee Williams attended University City High (long before my time and yours). But remember, creativity does not pertain only to those who see themselves as artists. We're all born creative. We use our creative skills every day as teachers, parents, friends, and colleagues. Continue to harness your imagination in whatever way you choose, and especially in your writing, whether you are penning articles for the Tom-Tom (the school newspaper), or writing an English essay on *Death of a Salesman*. Immerse yourself in stories. Keep reading novels. Spoiler alert: one day you will even write one!

#4. Move your body.

Jump. Dance. Hop. Canoe. Stretch. Immobility is not your friend. Okay...You were terrified of performing cartwheels in your high school production of Oklahoma. Get over it. Ultimately, your body doesn't know whether you are doing cartwheels across a stage or walking on a treadmill. It doesn't know if you are lifting a barbell or a bag of groceries. All your body knows is that it was made for movement. I advise you to follow Mom's example. Go watch her swim in that faded tank suit of hers, doing the front crawl, forty laps, three time a week. Study the arc of her arm as she lifts it out of the water, the bubbles gurgling from her mouth, the flutter of her kick; not a big splash, but a steady patter as her short muscular legs propel her up and down a single lane of the pool. This, sixteen-year-old Me, is your legacy. Her graceful strokes are your wings. Let the wind rise and carry you to new lands.

A Letter to My 16-Year-Old Self

by
Joanne Latimer

Dear 16-year-old self,

Well, it's been quite a year, hasn't it? A year of extremes. You are personally witnessing the clash between two of history's most powerful factions: disco and rock & roll. Your hormones are a rodeo bull tossing you upward into moments of sheer ecstasy, then yanking you into the depths of despair, throwing you sideways into dark bouts of rage, then crashing you flat into the ground to pick yourself up and start all over again. Your anthem switches from Janis Ian's "At Seventeen" to the Who's "My Generation" in the blink of an eye.

You're an extreme joiner – the school paper, the drama club, the folk group, a group that hands out leaflets protesting conditions for California Farm Workers, the library club – looking for somewhere to belong. (So many yearbook pictures). The only one of these you see through to the end, though, is the one with the fullest, most hardcore accountability: the school play. Don't sit that one out and forfeit the one thing that makes sense to you: the audience, the thrill of that moment when you and a room full of strangers come together in some strange and wonderful place and you're their guide through an unfamiliar world. The one place you get to be completely and unapologetically somebody else. Somebody else is easier, isn't it? Less confusing and troublesome. You were living for the day you turned sixteen. On that day, you stood in line at the Ministry of Transport to write the test for your 365, phase one of the much-coveted *driver's license*. This year, the world is opening up. Freshly independent with your new wheels (borrowed of course, on a strict schedule, from your

73

mother) but wheels nevertheless! The wheels are key, it seems. They take you places. The destination is not really the point—it's the getting away. Away from the growing chaos at home, the place where there is no corner to call your own. Every inch of space at home is shared, and you're learning to give over, to give in, and give up.

Chaos is a key theme for you, possibly because of the chaos in your head. Always a million ideas swirling into each other. There's a trail behind you of unfinished crafts, stories, projects. It's so hard to focus on one thing at a time and follow it through to its end. The only things you really manage to maintain in any kind of order are your school binders and notebooks. You've got dividers in there, dated class notes organized under neatly underlined headings with cogently fleshed out bullet lists. You haven't colour-coded anything, of course. That's just trying too hard.

At any rate, given that you're good with headings, I've organized this letter into a few. In each category is a list of things I think you need to hear:

Reasons you're likeable:

- You're funny. Yes, you do your little impromptu stand-up routines about the bus mishaps and your dog, but more than that, you're able to see the humour in situations and not take things too seriously. This will serve you very well in later years when things get difficult. They say that where there's laughter there's hope, and you will discover the truth in that during the darkest times when, instead of breaking down crying, you find yourself laughing at the absurdity of life and getting on with things. Humour is that one little green shoot growing out of the concrete. The indomitable force of life. Be sure to nurture it.
- You're smart. You catch onto things pretty quickly and that makes the world an interesting place for you. Just be careful. You still don't know everything although you seem fairly certain you do. Either that or it's important for you to make others think you do. Either way, it makes you a little insufferable at times. Keep that in check. The good news

is that you're smart enough to figure out that you still have a lot to learn, and so you will.

- You care about people. Once you call a person your friend, you will do whatever it takes to protect and support them. That's a reason to choose your friends more carefully. Be sure you choose people with the same quality to keep the balance even. Over the years, you will begin to value this quality over most others as you get to know people. You'll start to figure out that a person can have nothing else in common with you, but if they have a good heart you can be their friend.

Important things I need to set you straight about:
- You are not always right! Having said that, you'll start to understand that you often see things differently from the way the crowd sees them. I really want you to understand that just because a room full of people disagrees with you, it doesn't necessarily make you wrong. Remember the part about being smart? Well, it's not always about IQ. Smart can be about just taking the time to think through the details of things. Not everyone does that. If you've thought it through carefully enough, you could well be right. Trust your instincts and stick to your guns and don't take it personally when they tell you you're off base, or weird or wrong. This will become very important over the years.
- You *are* a good girl! Yeah, you're different from the other girls, but you've got it all mixed up. It's not about what the other girls have that you don't have. It's not that you're not quiet enough or pretty enough or thin enough or deferential enough. There are some things that you have that they don't have. You have a voice and things to say, you have physical presence and take up space, you have the power to make people laugh and maybe to think. These do not make you less of a girl. These are power tools that can make you a formidable woman. Don't tuck them away to settle for blending with the

75

others. See the reference to you vs. the roomful of people above.

Some Important Advice:

- Don't get that perm! I know you're a big fan of Harpo Marx, but you will regret looking like him for the next three months. Mark my words: cancel the hair appointment.
- Spend time with the people you love. Heads up: in a few short years, you will have one quiet, late-night talk over a cup of tea with your Irish grandmother who immigrated to New York at 18. She arrived in a new land with her husband and their handful of meager possessions, but without her first-born, your dad. On this night, you will learn some things about your culture, about your family, and about yourself. The most important lesson of these is this one, so remember it: this Irish woman, who personified the landscape in which she grew up, this immoveable rock from which sprang the green of life and love and joy, this woman who could see through artifice, and this woman, so wise, who all who knew her were afraid to cross for fear of that iron hand, will talk that night about her life as a young newlywed leaving a child behind to forge a new life with her husband. She will tell you about her helplessness when her mother-in-law declared that she "leave the boy," that it was out of her hands because "you didn't say no to that woman." In that moment it will become clear to you that this family matriarch who fills up a room with her presence and her power was once young, unsure, afraid to argue. Look at who she is now. Know that her blood is in your veins. I urge you to embrace that truth and see how powerful you can be. Don't be afraid of it and by all means, don't be afraid of upsetting people with it. And spend more time with this woman. That quiet little heart to heart with her will be the last one you get.
- Don't be so well behaved. Stop trying to be less rebellious and find a productive outlet for your rebellion. I read

once that no well-behaved woman ever made history. Put that on a plaque and mount it on your wall.

- Trust your instincts.

Apologies: (I definitely owe you some)
- I am sorry I didn't value you enough back then to draw lines and ask for what you needed.
- I'm sorry that I didn't stand up for you when you needed it and that when I became angry with the world I took it out on you. I'm working on making it up to you now.
- I'm sorry I didn't love you very much. I'm lately working on learning how.

All headings aside, I'll warn you that you will let your greatest passion, theatre and acting, slide to the side of the road for a long time. Try not to be too hard on yourself about it. There are all kinds of factors that will contribute to its neglect and you won't own all of them. Blaming yourself will just make going back to get it harder. The good news is that you will find your way back to it in a meaningful way and you will appreciate the gift of it all the more for having lost it for a time.

I should also let you know that despite your vow never to get married, you will. Full disclosure, it will not end well, but the upside is that it will bring two new highly creative, interesting wonderful, and very different human beings into your life. You have no way right now to fathom what this means, but raising your daughter and your son will be the biggest challenge you will ever face. You'll have no idea what you're doing, and just when you start to think you do, they'll change it up on you. They will make you feel stupid and beautiful and powerful and helpless. Trust your instincts, though. They will serve you well. Remember what I told you about your grandmother? It turns out that this is where all her strength came from. It's also the source of so much joy.

The important thing I really want you to know is that the whole experience is up to you. Decide what you want. You do deserve it, but it won't fall into your lap. Go after it. Buckle up, embrace the journey, and hang in there.

Your friend,

An older, (slightly wiser), Joanne.

A Letter to My 16-Year-Old Self

by
Josée Sigouin

My dear Josée,

What I remember most clearly about being sixteen is wondering who I was and who I would become. The answer seems quite simple now, plain to see in the books you read, the music you listen to, what you write and even what you draw.

At twelve, you devoured the collected works of Jules Verne. At sixteen you were into Emile Zola: thick tomes, complex stories, vivid descriptions and thought-provoking scenes. Passion. Social commentary on class differences and, most of all, heroines who will settle for nothing but what is real and what is just. The novels are not what your friends read and they are not, God forbid, required reading at school. The nuns frown on Monsieur Zola. His books are branded as immoral by the Church. Immoral? Well, yes, Nana, the man-eater will be immoral when you get around to reading her story, but not Angélique in *The Dream* with her religious zeal, not Catherine who toils in the coalmines of *Germinal*, and certainly not Denise, who works at, *The Ladies' Paradise*, a department store to feed her two brothers.

Just as books are an integral part of your life, so is music. Switch on the radio and before the afternoon is over, I'm sure you will turn up the volume for Chicago's "Color My World," with its dreamy romanticism, and "Lay Lady Lay" by Dylan, with its troubling invitation and equally troubling tenderness. You will get up from your chair and waltz to "What the World Needs Now," but when the DJ plays "Ball of Confusion," you will hold your breath to try and follow the rapid-fire lyrics.

You are the sum of these books and songs, by turns idealistic, optimistic, individualistic, passionate, confused and, most of all, romantic. You are in love with the idea of love and yet as uncompromising as Zola's heroines. Your brothers say that no one will ever be interested in you. Sweet sixteen and never been kissed. Well, never mind that silly saying. Do you remember a drawing you made in grade four? You still have it somewhere, I am sure. Look for a young man with a foreign slant to his eyes, The Jade Prince, named for the shade of Prismacolor you used for his jacket. Figment of your imagination, or premonition? All I can say is that your brothers will eat their words.

People say many things about words, that they have the power to destroy and heal, and the power to change the world. You wrote: *Les mots vous livrent et vous délivrent*. Words betray you; they set you free. In French, livre also means book: Words "book" you and "un-book" you, or something to that effect.

You have tinkered with the idea of writing a book but it is such a monumental task that you have abandoned each attempt after only a few chapters. How do real writers do it? My sense is that they are, or were, geniuses. In 2014—such is progress—we have personal computers and we use them for computing, yes, but also for writing. I have written this letter not on a typewriter, as might appear to you, but on a computer, and I can tell you this: it may look nice and polished but I have re-written at least one word out of every three. I have moved text around. I have deleted whole sentences and brought them back after realizing that they were needed after all.

That said, a computer does not a writer make, and you are fated to walk a different path ... for a time. What that path is, I will let you discover, but one day, many years from now, something unexpected will happen. It will start innocently enough with a television series that never would have come to your

80

attention if not for your best friend, your lover, your husband, your Jade Prince, who, incidentally comes from Hong Kong. The year is 2005, and a portion of the world is captivated by the trials and tribulations of a semi-fictitious woman named Jang Geum who lived in sixteenth-century Korea. She is everything Zola's heroines were, and more.

Jang Geum will be just the beginning. By the time you write this letter you will have logged over 4,000 hours absorbing what makes the people of South Korea sweat, swear, and shed tears, through books, magazines, film, and television. You will have learned some basic Korean and visited the country twice. And for the past seven years, you will have been writing a novel set in Korea. It is a monumental task, no question about it: a journey fraught with contrary winds, course changes and bodies thrown overboard, otherwise known as killing your darlings.

How does it end? I don't know. I'm not there yet. All I can say is that it's worth every second spent navigating the rocky shoals of mixed metaphors, telling rather than showing, tired clichés and the dreaded adverbs that others *kindly* point out are "not needed." At times it is worse than rolling a boulder up a hill but at other times the story seems to write itself. You are merely a conduit. Your characters – your creations! – take you in directions that you had never imagined. Links are forged that you never intended. And they seem so right, so inevitable.

See how I get carried away! Writer's high.

But now it is time to say Goodbye. I wanted to tell you what I thought you longed to know—who you were, whether you'd find love, what you would become. I see now that it's the other way around. You are the one who told me, reminded me, what I longed to know. *Les mots vous livrent et vous délivrent.* Words have betrayed me by telling the world who I am, and freed me to be myself: idealistic, optimistic, individualistic, romantic, confused, and, most of all, passionate.
Thank you. Yours, José

A Letter to My 16-Year-Old Self

by
Karine Silverwoman

When I was 18-years-old, I was charged with 17 million dollars worth of damage to the government. I am not kidding. I would say that the "being at the wrong place at the wrong time" cliché was accurate in this situation. Now that I have a daughter, I pray to god she doesn't do half of the things that I did.

Bless my parents.

I did not do the crime I was charged with. I did other crimes but not that one. When I was arrested, I was put in the back of a van with four male police officers, driven to the 52nd division on Dundas Street, handcuffed, and put in a cell for 15 hours before being spoken to at all. To distract myself, I tried to recite every Robert Munsch story I could remember from when I was a child: *50 Below Zero, Paper Bag Princess, I Love You Forever*. It made me feel safe and innocent. I was innocent.

When I was arrested, I had French braid pigtails with a shaved undercut, heavy eyeliner overshadowing insecurities, black carhartt overall pants with a skull patch sewn on, and steel-toed army boots, Sharpie in hand and the most dogmatic chants in my back pocket ready to whip out like a Bible. I looked like Anne Frank as a punk, with big hoop earrings, reading the holy scriptures of Ani Difranco and memorizing the poetics of Audre Lorde. I was at the height of my feminist awakening, and my goal was to smash the patriarchy with my bare hands. Again, blaming my parents would be convenient, but now that I am a mother, I am more cautious of these linkages.

My parents were also activists. They had alias names and were staunch Maoists waiting for the revolution that was not around the corner. They were selling communist manifesto newspapers full time until I was seven-years-old. When I kept coming home from dates dissatisfied, it was my parents who suggested that perhaps I was a lesbian. They were right. They grew this seed of justice inside of me and have been watering this rage with tenderness and care. Perhaps they envisioned me writing letters to the editor or signing petitions rather than getting charged with 17 million dollars worth of damage to the government.

18 was an explosive time. When you feel immortal, you act immortal. My uncertainties were at a crossroads with my new position as a know-it-all adult. I no longer crossed my arms over my belly and slouched through the city. Unfolding, I was rough around the edges, wanting to fall into the world, yet my close companion – anxiety – followed me like a quiet wind. I felt the world could topple me.

Hour 10 at the 52nd division: I start thinking about how my parents sent me to a psychiatrist at SickKids hospital. I had refused to talk. I had wanted to tell the psychiatrist about the time when my grandpa, the most jovial, softest man on the planet, stopped the car and cried on the steering wheel when I told him I had German friends. I was seven. I had wanted to tell her about my mom begging me to do yoga because she said I had to find my breath. I had wanted to tell her I didn't know where my breath was. That it was missing, that I didn't have the tools to find it. Instead, the psychiatrist and I would face each other for an hour while I would stare and criticize her fashion choices from head to toe in silence, then leave.

At 18, I still left scissors at my bedside window in case I needed to cut the screen door open and escape. I was afraid of the dark and basements, yet I would be the first at a barricade protest line. I was ashamed of my body but I was the first to turn spin the bottle into a game of strip poker with all the polyamorous punks. I wanted to be loved by one person so badly, but monogamy was a symptom of the state.

It was at 18 when the lines of right and wrong were becoming blurry. Some experiences quiet you. When I was arrested and brought to the station, a lesbian cop stripped searched me and left the door open for the male officers to see. I had barely stood naked for a lover. There was something so reassuring about the world when it was cut into simple halves of evil and good. Capitalism and men were bad, and the activist and the struggle were good. These binaries and this meaning was my driving force. I had found the answer to fill every existential hole. With pride and fury, I held the ultimate truths in my back pocket.

It was not my hefty, serious charges that altered me completely, but rather the aftermath, the political repercussions, the new perspective I had of my community and, ultimately, my sacred truths being shattered before my 18-year-old eyes. I had always come to expect violence and unfair treatment from the state. I expected it and I searched for it—it was practically all I saw. In this singular vision I was not attuned to the inner politics of community activism, the in-fighting, the machismo and, following my arrest, the feelings of loneliness. After I got charged, I was not allowed to go to protests anymore, and thus was not seen by the popular activists as valued or of worth. I was to suck it up. This breaking open of complexities was not an easy process.

After 15 hours alone in the cell, I was allowed to pee and was then taken to a room where I was told to sit on a red fabric loveseat. I was interrogated by two officers in plain clothes. I was absolutely terrified, but I did everything to hide that. It was at this moment that I wished I had had taken my mom's advice and gone to yoga. Where was my breath? I had my arms stretched out over the chair while questions were fired at me. I was Teflon. I was unbreakable. I was 18.

"Do you understand that you are in very big trouble?"

"Do you understand you could rot in jail?"

"Do your parents approve of your criminal behavior? Would your parents mind if we searched their entire house? How about if we round up your friends?"

"I wish to remain silent," is all I said to them. Over and over. "I wish to remain silent." I must have said it 30 times. "I wish to remain silent." My heart was pounding so hard that I was sure they could hear it. But my face and my stance didn't waver. My chest was puffed out; I could walk out of here and rob ten banks, and chain myself to something. Nothing could crack me. Not this police station, not this interrogation, not these charges.

The police had insisted I stay in jail until my trial. They said I was a danger to society. I looked over at my parents in the courtroom. My feet and hands were cuffed. I wanted to cuddle with them and watch *Seinfeld* in bed. They say one hour in jail is like one day. So 24 days later I was released. When I was finally free to go, my parents touched my arm and asked, "Are you okay?"

"Hold on," I said, "I just need to catch my breath."

SEASON 3: PART FIVE

A LETTER TO MY QUEER FAMILY
(TORONTO WORLD PRIDE EVENT)
June 22, 2014

Katerina Cook

Farzana Doctor

Mary Ellen Maclean

Karleen Pendleton Jimenez

A Letter to My Queer Family

by
Katerina Cook

Dear Mom, Dad, Karleen, Fran, Carter and Elena,

I love you. Elena, you are the cutest four-and-a-half year-old ever. I miss you so much when I'm at my dad's house. I want to pick you up and hold you. I will read you as many books and sing you as many songs as you want. Carter, I miss you too sometimes, but you haven't been in university long enough for me to want you back just yet. I would say give it another year, but by then I might be in university too. I hope you become the best video game designer the world has ever seen.

Dear audience,

I live two lives. One at Mom's house, and one at Dad's. I don't see how Mom and Dad could ever have been together. Dad lives in a world of wine and cheese and, "Did you have a nice day at work?" Mom lives in a world of rights and freedoms and memories. Dad does not live in the past, though he doesn't seem to be moving forward, either. It is very rare that I can wheedle out a family tale, which I am so interested in hearing. But the house seems stagnant to me. New stove, new job, but always the same conversation. Opinions only on best software, best sausage; nothing on politics, art, culture. I starve for opinions and observations when I'm at my dad's. Maybe all teenagers feel that way about their parents. Yet I feel and sometimes glimpse another person behind my dad who has a lot to say and care about. I see it in the simple music he learns on the piano, the Joni Mitchell on the stereo, and in his fantastic movie collection, from

Blade Runner to *Annie Hall*. Just from that we seem finally related, but in person, we just can't understand each other.

Dear Dad,

You keep your life and personality behind a mask. I wonder how long ago that mask has been in place. I guess sixteen years ago when Mom broke up with you. That would be the very dramatic explanation, and yet there must be one. I think you are much more yourself when Fran is not around. I do not begrudge you being with Fran, I think she makes you happy. But I wonder why you feel you cannot be honest around me, or for all I know with yourself.

Dear Mom,

As you well know, I am almost seventeen now. I don't know how that looks to you but I feel very old. People keep asking me what I want to do—lawyer, musician, I don't know. I can't even understand who I am. One thing that grounds me, though, is that I am my mother's daughter. I seem to have inherited your taste in clothes (long, pleated skirts and channel jackets), and your passion for books (Charlotte Bronte and Colette basically shaped my outlook on life), but I don't seem to have your knack for making things, clothes, tools etc. I have latched on to your identity, looking at your past and present, to guess at my future. But even before I started this quest for my identity, there was always one trait I claimed proudly: You were a lesbian. I'm not sure how early I became aware of this. You told me that when Carter and I were little, we hatched plans to get rid of Karleen and get you back with Dad, but we would have done that whichever gender Dad's replacement had been. I do remember the pride, fear, and anger I felt having two moms. Never anger at you, but at the kids in class at school who would unwittingly say, "That's so gay." It was a personal attack. You just insulted my mother. That's worse than insulting me. They had not anticipated the swear words I had ready for them, learned from when you accidentally cut your thumb.

I was proud of your being a lesbian. To me, that was defiance and strength. But I was scared of what others would think. I knew people thought being gay was weird or gross. Sometimes, when I made a new friend, I would avoid saying "my moms" for a while, or at all. I was ashamed of hiding it, which just added to my anger. But sometimes I would say it just to judge whether they were worthy of being my friend. If they didn't say something stupid about it, they were all right by me. I got crushes on girls and boys in elementary school (I had a girlfriend briefly in grade four) but I don't know if all kids are like that, or whether I was just more prone to acknowledge it because of having two moms or what. I think everyone is a little bit gay.

There are great parts about being part of the Queer community, too. Gay parties are a lot more fun than straight parties (there's more dancing for one thing). I don't know how long I can mooch off my parents' gayness to attend queer events. "I have two moms" is no longer a sufficient reply when someone asks you how you fit in. Luckily I seem to be truly bisexual, but what if I wasn't? Am I no longer part of the community? Because the gay community is the one in which I feel most at home. It is my community. Thanks for giving a white girl a cause. And thanks for the great gaydar.

A Letter to My Queer Family

by
Farzana Doctor

My Dear One,

You don't remember this, but
You asked me to dance
At the Ottawa gay centre
You pulled me in close
I wasn't sure where to put my hands

When the song ended
I was all blushing twenty-two-ness
You called me Vishnu
Mistaking my pinking brown skin
For light blue.
Still I quietly crushed over you

I didn't mean for this to be an angry letter.

In Toronto
We met again at a
Women's (spelled with a 'y')
Discussion circle
You sat at twelve o'clock
So I took the chair at six

The topic that day
Was bisexuals and disease and fences
So I followed
What I thought were your customs

Brush-cut my long waves
Bought a lumber-jack jacket
Came out as a lesbian

I told everyone I thought
Penises were weird
Which was true, but not quite

I didn't mean for this to be a confused letter?

I could tell you liked me
At least a little
When you suggested
I join your committee
I stayed up all night painting banners
Hoisted them high
In your marches

And then one night
It happened
(you tell it differently, but I don't mind)
It was too late to go home
You shared your bed
Just to sleep, you said

Your lips were as soft as I'd imagined
Your fingers reached inside me
Claimed me
I'm yours, I pledged
A half-whisper in the dark

Soon, we were contemplating babies
(my eggs, your womb, some guy's sperm)
Buying a cottage on a secret lake
Adopting a rescue dog
Were perfectly lesbian

I thought you'd be more proud of me

When I organized radical potlucks
And made films
Wrote plays,
The spotlight shifting
I admit, I liked its brightness

Two years later,
You said things change
We changed
I agreed to disagree
My heart an aching muscle.

I'd once wanted this to be a love letter.

2 years, then 5, now 15
Chosen family is better than nothing
You and I fell in and out of love and lust
With other women
We bought condos, and duplexes
Adopted more rescue dogs

The laws we'd protested died
And you married one of my exes
I was mostly happy for you but
Quietly complained about
Heteronormativity
Instead of broken promises

I didn't mean to make this letter all about me.

I'm not sure when it happened
The tremor
That shifted the ground beneath me
Maybe it was hormones
Maybe it was astrology
Maybe it was that I allowed dudes
To join my collective
Maybe it's that I never truly

Believed in fences

Over coffee I told you
Gender is fluid
Desire a construction
And penises?
(Just inside out vaginas!)
You frowned in confusion
Your critique
A hushed version
Of the scorn I one leveled
At all those queer Desi girls
Who married boys and
Disappeared into the suburbs

I haven't

I haven't
Left the city
But you no longer
Invite me to your house

The last time we passed
In the street
A year ago
I called out
And you blinked and squinted
It took you a moment
To recognize
My queer body

I meant for this to be a queer letter.

A Letter to My Queer Family

by
Mary Ellen Maclean

Dear Queer Family,

At 50, I never, never, never, never, never, never, never thought I would be married. As a younger queer gal hailing from the East Coast of this great country of ours, and a recovering Catholic, my response to the idea of marriage was: "No way, that's such a patriarchal set up, it's so not me, what the hell do I need to be married for? That's just so... straight." Well...never say never, because here I am very happily married to you, Wendy, who somehow found me four years ago at a hockey tournament in Iceland, of all places. The land of fire and ice took on a whole new meaning and will forever be burned and frozen (in a good way) into my being. You and the girls, Olivia, (25), Amelia (18), and Ruby (10), (who said to me this morning, "I've been in a queer family my whole life!") and cat Tiger, the male of the house, and our newest member Jett the girl dog, make up our family.

My path to you, dear family, started right from the get-go as a little Mary Ellen with excellent gaydar (**gay-dar**: *sixth sense of being able to detect if someone is gay, lesbian, queer without them telling you*). My gaydar was tuned in at the age of seven. I knew then I belonged to not only my great family: Mum, Dad, and my four siblings who have embraced me always, but also to another kind of family.

My Dad was in the army and we were posted to Cornwallis, Nova Scotia—an army recruit training base with family living quarters. I was involved in many activities: hockey (the only girl in the whole province); and Brownies (I refused to wear the skirt protesting that it wasn't fair and, "How are you supposed to climb and do handstand in a skirt!?"). They had to change the rules, and I stand proudly in my crimplean brown slacks in those 1970s photos. My favourite activity was sneaking into the off-limits obstacle course for the recruits-in-training. I was banned from the area. It was dangerous, apparently, for an eight-year old to be climbing 12-foot wooden walls and rope bridges 40-feet in the air. I didn't understand what the issue was. Because I needed lots of activities to keep me out of the obstacle course, I was put into day camps and over-night camps. There were two women who were leaders of the camp, one year. They made my gaydar go off immediately, and I remember looking at them and knowing they were like me. I just knew, somehow. I couldn't wait to be old enough to have girlfriends like them.

After that first decade of knowing there were more of me out there, more that were part of this kind of family I didn't quite know how to name, I entered junior high and met my gym teacher, Debby Dunham. The gaydar went off big time and she always made me feel like I wasn't alone in this other kind of family. She never said anything directly—it was just a knowing, a way of being comfortable. She coached me to throw the discus for track and field. I broke the record and still hold it to this day, (I'll be damned if I can remember the distance). After I won, I ran up to Debby Dunham hugged her and said, "I broke the fucking record." She told me years later she never had a kid swear like that with such joy...she hugged me back. She has shown up at many of my shows over the years. She's a member of my queer family that I will always remember.

In high school, I hung out with a band of lesbians, gays and bisexuals who found our home bases in the drama club, choir, school musicals and sports teams. My queerness was diverse: I liked athletics, theatre, and getting into bars under age, (at which our gang was very good). We were a family of misfits, and it didn't occur to us to be anything other than who we were. I'm still connected to some of these folks—these family members.

After busting out of high school, I embarked on forming a theatre company – Jest in Time Theatre - and started touring across Canada. I had two jobs then: performing and searching for gay bars everywhere I went, from urban cities like Toronto to tiny tiny towns in Saskatchewan. I came across some real winners, which is a whole other story. During those years, I found many dark alleys, black painted doors, books you had to sign to get into the dimly lit, badly furnished basement bars with no air and lots of cigarette smoke. But these places had family members in them, and I was fascinated by it all.

In my third decade, I started touring internationally with the company and I was exposed to a whole new world where the black alley doorways were replaced with open patios and big bright signs and all kinds of happy people—happy, gay people! Oh, what fun to walk into a club in Sydney, Australia and feel like I was home somehow with a knowing family. During this third decade, I got into a long-term relationship. This family included a partner, three cats, a house, a dog, a cottage, and lawnmowers. Our home was a drop-in centre for those queer family members who needed a place to feel at home. That was a rotating family full of comings and goings. The third decade ended with that family breaking apart and me with it. I'm happy to say I'm friends with that ex-partner which is not always the case. She's remained family.

The fourth decade was about learning what family really was—and boy, did I get that mixed up sometimes. I decided to move from Halifax to Toronto, "for a while," to change things up a bit. Well, that turned out to be an understatement. I'm married now, a parent, I have a new house and a new dog! But, no lawnmowers...yet.

I have been privileged to have a bigger queer family my whole life, just like Ruby, and the freedom to celebrate that in this country. For this I'm grateful. But finding you, Wendy, Olivia, Amelia, Ruby, Tiger the boy cat and Jett the girl dog is the best thing. My family. I don't feel like I have to single out my family as my queer family. You are my family. I've learned that our families come in many shapes, sizes, sexes, colours, ages, races, combinations—it's all how one sees it, lives it and, most importantly, enjoys and loves it.

So I guess this is a love letter to you dear ones. I love my family, all of them.

Best,

Mary Ellen

A Letter to My Queer Family

by
Karleen Pendleton Jimenez

Dear Mom,

I know you thought it wasn't your fault, me coming out gay, that I was born this way, and I probably was. But damn, I loved it on school mornings when you let me climb into your bed while you got ready. I loved watching you put your bra on, and your silky shirts. I loved when you pulled your nylons up your big soft legs. I loved the spray of the opium perfume filling the room. The gentle touches of your fingers shaping your perm. It's been 30 years since then, but when I think of wanting a woman, I still think of those mornings together in your bedroom.

Dear Dad,

I received your card and photos last month. Thanks for the mother's day wishes. You looked fabulous in the new black skirt and royal-blue blouse I got you for your 80th birthday. You hold your hand up behind your head, chest out, flamboyantly displaying the length of your smooth suntanned neck, and the bulges of your satin breasts. The woman at the mall did a good job on your makeup, the blush drawing out your round, glowing cheeks, the eyeliner highlighting your blue-gray eyes. It's exciting for you to send the photos of yourself. You need to share your beautiful, decorated body with me and anyone else who might look. I sense your anticipation of a joy in that sharing that you never quite experience. You keep trying though, hoping with each parade past a sales girl that the longing will be fulfilled.

I know it doesn't matter now. What's done is done. But I can't help wondering if you could have been a better man if that little boy who snuck into his mother's makeup kit in the 1930s had been cherished.

Dear Girlfriend,

You were with a computer guy who felt secure through marriage vows and monogamy. You gave it up for an angsty butch writer who wanted to get a PhD. You decided to be my lover and make a family with me. That's a big deal. I have been told by my exes that I looked too queer, too boyish, to be with forever after, or even the morning after.

You build a solid home for us, sanding wood cutting boards, scratching old paint from the walls, surrounding us with purple peonies and red maple. You couldn't sit still if you tried.

Thank god you can't cook, so there is a role left for me. I love being the chemist in the kitchen, concocting recipes from what's left in the fridge: mango penne, rainbow trout kale enchiladas, burgers, smoothies, quesadillas. I relish feeding you, watching you eat my offering—it feels like love to me.

Dear Mother-in-law,

You weren't so sure at first about this lesbian stealing away your daughter. And yet by the time I was asking Canada to let me stay here with her, you wrote the longest letter of support, including: "She's a wonderful third parent for my grandchildren and a loving supportive partner for my child."

When you were a little girl, you hung with a pack of boys, and grew into a woman journalist adventurer who demanded life on your own terms. Maybe that's why you could see the value in our queerness, in two women breaking convention, reserving our love for one another. I enjoy your enthusiasm for lesbians at large, like our heated texting celebration last week upon witnessing Kathleen (Wynne) and Jane on-stage, pearls aside.

But I most enjoy our sneaky scotch-on-the-rocks on the back patio on a late Sunday afternoon with crackers, hot stuff, and family gossip.

Dear daughter Katie, almost 17-years-old,

Every time I heard about a kid or a teacher throwing a homophobic line your way I felt rage and helplessness. I can bear the homophobia thrown at me. I can step right back into the perpetrator's face and educate them. But I can't bear them hurting you. When you were in the 4th grade, I think you were running the anti-homophobia training for teachers and administrators at your school. You shouldn't have had to do that.

You've become a powerhouse who will go off to university in a year's time. I could speak of all your accomplishments, but you will do so yourself in another moment (See Katerina Cook's letter in this collection). Suffice to say that you have all my admiration.

Dear daughter Elena, almost five-years-old,

Every single time you wear your sparkly outfits, where glitter and polkadots are involved, people on the streets make comments about you. "Wow, what a girly girl! She's so precious. Look at those silver shoes!" And sometimes the comments feel warm and supportive, but sometimes they feel heavy and sinister, and you can feel it too and retreat behind one of my legs. You've got good instincts.

As a tomboy, I never heard these comments. There is an intensity and repetition involved in response to a young girl's vibrant femininity. It's kind of frightening.

In my queer family, you can choose pink and purple, you can wave your four-year-old bum around to Lady Gaga songs, you can have gender and sexuality however you like it.

SEASON 4: PART ONE

A LETTER TO THE ROAD I DIDN'T TRAVEL
October 19, 2014

Amanda Greer

Tanya Neumeyer

Alicia Payne

A Letter to the Road I didn't Travel

by
Amanda Greer

Dear musician, singer, actress, doctor, scientist, spy, and Hogwarts student,

All of you are part of my past. You were all part of me at some point or other, dreams which, with the childish expectancy of a great destiny, I always thought would become reality. (Even though I knew that Hogwarts was fictional, I was still terribly disappointed when my eleventh birthday came and went without an acceptance letter).

As a kid, I prided myself on my 10-year plans and my meticulous To-Do lists. I was a juvenile neurotic. ("I'm going to get my PhD by the time I'm 25," I remember saying to my mother after a music lesson, around age 10). I wouldn't be surprised if she watched Woody Allen's entire body of work while I was in utero.

Luckily for my anxious tendencies, I managed to avoid a mid-childhood crisis by discovering at an early age what I considered the only road worth travelling: music. I asked my parents to put me in piano lessons, then violin lessons, then singing. I joined orchestras, choirs, bands. There's nothing like playing with other people—the energy and sound, the energy of the sounds, enveloping you. As the music swirls around you, you begin to feel part of something that's bigger than yourself.

Sadly, I didn't want to be part of something bigger than myself; I wanted *myself* to be bigger than myself. I wanted to be great. Heading into middle school, I devoted more and more time to singing. Singing was personal. Violin and piano, as instruments, separate you from the audience. Singing requires you to put *yourself* on display. "You are your voice, and your voice is your instrument," one of my singing teachers used to say. This terrified me. My adolescent neuroses reacted violently against the whole idea. But I saw the reward. When you sang, people paid attention. In middle school, I was never the centre of anything. The centre, just like with any teen comedy, was made up of athletes. I would stand on the fringes and look in at them, comparing my pubertal awkwardness to their impossible ease. I'd gotten curves before the other girls, and had an unfortunate attachment to Avril Lavigne concert t-shirts, studded chokers, and camouflage-patterned cargo shorts. My favourite movies were the *Lord of the Rings* films (I had once delivered a speech on J. R.R Tolkien to the class in Elvish), and I quoted Monty Python like it was 1975. Needless to say, standing next to the petite, perpetually tanned girls who played hockey and soccer and joked effortlessly with the boys, I felt like a pimply nerd stuck in a vortex of all things uncool. But there was something that I could do that they could not—sing.

I began to fantasize about becoming a star. When I heard that some singers were discovered singing in public places, I began humming under my breath in stores and restaurants, hoping that one day, a record executive would hear me and go: "Gee, listen to that voice! Get her a contract—this kid'll be a star!" (In my head, everyone spoke like they were in a 1930s backstage musical). When my classmates teased me for liking Avril Lavigne, I'd silently practice my Tony acceptance speech. When I found out that a boy I liked had a crush on a perky girl I'd always been conflictingly envious and hateful of, I just said, "Well, one day I'll be a Broadway star, *and then they'll be sorry!*"

In the middle of grade eight, I got my "big break." I was accepted into the Etobicoke School of the Arts for musical theatre. I spent the summer beforehand walking on air, elated to be getting out of my athleticized middle school and into a society of sensitive, *cultured* 14-year-olds.

It didn't turn out quite like I'd expected.

At a dress rehearsal for one of the musicals I was in, a teacher told a girl over the loudspeaker that her leotard was "totally unflattering," humiliating her in front of our entire grade.

For one of our dance exams, another teacher told the girls to show up in bras and booty shorts. We protested. This teacher, who wore stilettos to class almost every day, told us that we should be professionals. When we pointed out that the boys didn't have to show up to our exam dressed like that, she just said: "That's the way it is in the real world." She seemed to have forgotten we were only 15.

A classical singer, I also didn't fit the mold of a Broadway diva. My teachers at school told me that they simply didn't know what to do with me. I began to turn to opera as a career. I was determined that someday, I'd sing to audiences of thousands, (every member of which would probably be over the age of 60). I even went to opera camp in New York. It was there that I got to work with a singer from the Met. He told me he liked me, and invited me to study with him.

He also asked me if I wanted a family someday.

I said yes.

"You're in the wrong career for that," he told me. He seemed sorry about it. "You'll move around from place to place – wherever there's work – and there'll be months when you won't be working at all. It's an unpredictable life, and a hard one," he finished.

I went away from my meeting with him with my head feeling like it was full of television static. I had always known that being a performer was a difficult life. I had also always known that I wanted a family, and a home, and, (because my childhood neuroses hadn't entirely gone away with age), stability.

That fall, I switched high schools, and began a (brief) flirtation with the possibility of medical school. I never looked back, but lately I've begun to think about what might have been.

If I had continued singing, where would I be going to school? Would I be doing well? Would I be crying on the phone to my mother every night?

If, back in eighth grade, I had chosen the violin instead of singing, would I be getting ready to audition for a philharmonic?

Would I be on Cape Breton Island, fiddling at *ceidlidhs*? Would I have quit, even then?

What I've realized, though – and it's taken the four years I've spent away from most music performance to get to this point – is that greatness doesn't mean having millions of fans. In middle school, I think I needed singing. I needed to know that I was worth something. But now, now I have friends and family who show me I'm worth something every day.

I'm about to graduate from university. I'm at a point in my life when there are infinite roads that I could travel. Infinite possibilities. Infinite destinies. Infinite choose-your-own-adventures. It's intimidating, but I'm surprisingly calm. I know that, whatever I choose and whatever chooses me, greatness doesn't lie in monumental achievements. Greatness is standing by a friend when the rest of the world's against them. Greatness is raising a kid so that they grow up to be a pretty cool and mostly normal adult. Greatness is finding a lifelong husband or wife to share in the adventure with you. Greatness is changing someone's life, even just slightly, for the better. Contrary to Shakespeare's theory, we are all born great. And I think it's time that we realized it.

A Letter to the Road I didn't Travel

by
Tanya Neumeyer

I am a poet
and I might not have been
if I had traveled the roads mapped out for me

poet: community builder, educator
a trembling mix of passion and fear
that courses through my body from first performances to my still
racing heart
honest about the ways I am tender, fragile and vulnerable
I am strengthened in this truth-telling

to the road I travel called poet – full of possibility
there is a kind of proof here, an example of what others can also
do
I come out of what holds me back
from being the best of myself
I embrace my strengths, weaknesses, imperfections and rather-
be-hidden parts
I bring all of my light woven in darkness to meet the world

because I come face to face with what Audre Lorde describes
as
the fear of that "visibility without which we cannot truly live"
and I know that such fear is only broken by speaking

I must tell you this:
in the silence of where I come from
with what sets me into trouble, chaos and creativity

with what helps me feel more free
and leads me on a path of growth
I am learning to live well in this world
I have learned by making tough choices
and that has made all the difference

to the road I didn't travel called engineering
I will not give you my everything in exchange for nothing
I need the right road for me
even though I know you're amazing, like the rock cycle
where rock becomes sediment, and sediment becomes rock
and rock is metamorphosed
transforming in shape, colour and form
even at its most basic unit
the most obvious of unbelievable change takes place
I too change metamorphically
as wind and water wear down my hard rocky layers over time
there's a lifetime of work here

I am transformation beyond imagination
rock on and beautiful
and I know now that stained glass is only born of silica put
together in the right way

to the road I didn't travel called not breathing
you are not an option I chose

to the road I didn't travel called cycles of violence
forget you, I'm finished
I don't want to live as an animal in that cage clawing out my
own eyes
I am the bull and the china shop
I've got loving and living and healing to do
though sometimes I wonder
where I would be without loving, adoptive parents
who gave me space to grow

I've struggled, and I struggle still

but now my strength helps others too
as fragile as I am, I am strong

but Joan,
Joan, had 3 children, out of wedlock
always wondering if this was wise, because of their father
in a family, where the father pushes the mother from a moving
vehicle
there is a kind of turmoil that activates a system
made to protect children
so it was
Joan's children were endlessly not her own

where is the healing in this?
strain to hear it, expect it in despair, in the depths of difficulty
it's in the sound of rising above
and rise above, I must
I see the life I might have lived
impoverished by my poorly thought out actions, by impulses
conditioned by the path of my youthful world
I was lawless, reckless
and in charge of myself

Joan is my biological mother
and my biological father is too much to tell you about
I was a young person who had too many burdens too soon
too much responsibility for my two younger siblings too much of
the time
my mother didn't have the life skills necessary to raise us
she coped long enough to keep us together for a short time
before my father would come back into the picture

I lived a young life with moments of immersion in cultures
I didn't want to emulate
but the Children's Aid Society, a women's shelter, police,
lawmakers, friends
and families intervened to change the course of things for me
to help me see

that was not a road I wanted to travel

my family has so many branches
that I've wandered down branched roads
until it's hard to see where I've come from
but looking back I see
the road I didn't travel called being my parents' child

to that road
I take only the gifts, I leave behind the disasters

it takes courage to leave
to depart from what is known
I know what I've left behind:

it's my hope for a better past
too many garbage bags
a business plan
a best-friends-forever-ship
a real mom
a birthright
bright eyes, clear seeing, self being
16 brick houses, one with my name still etched in chalk 14 years
later
I still carry too much fear

I've left behind everything
but a tiny blue duffle bag
a story book and a red hearted shirt

I've left behind my family of chaos, of origin, of biology
I've left behind whole lives in Brantford, Bradford, Hamilton,
Whitby
Scarborough, Newmarket, India and Cuba
with my heart in a suitcase, my emotions in a bag
I still long for, and feel the loss of, that sense of family
I witness as commonplace for others
when I feel broken, I work constantly on healing

I'm open about where I've come from
curiously active, and growing into the future
keeping the strengths I already have
moving through what darkness remains
and when I find you here, you – that road that I want, I need,
the one I aim for and am encouraged to travel on
I write, as a poet
about how before my mother gave me to her sister
she told me:

be careful, watch out
this shattered glass life has sharp edges
still I grew to walk through the world
bright blue eyes dancing from light shining within
but the edge of this broken glass world gets too close
it cuts, it hurts
more than numbness and fear
more than worry and expectation

I wait, beg for the kind of healing
that is carefully picking up the shards
placing them attentively in a frame
cementing them there
waiting, for that stained glass holy birth moment
when I will hold my masterpiece up to the light
and let it shine through, poet

but still there are days when I heave sighs
that tell you I'm from somewhere else
I long to blend in
I'm good at it
it's easy to assume I'm a girl from up the street

where I live now people worry about hills and fuel prices
my family mistakes me for their own child
I catch myself before speaking otherwise
my disguise is instinct
I need to belong

I've abandoned the life I once lived
it is no longer
my only option is to make this work
pay attention
dress like them
live like them
walk like them
I make my life revealing little
the sole bearer of my true story
but sometimes you can catch me breathing so deeply
you might wonder where I come from

the ocean swells within me
calls me back
threatens to drown me
do you know the cost of breathing once the ocean has made its
way in?

to all the roads I didn't travel
your lessons have been invaluable
and "knowing how way leads on to way" as Frost so aptly put it

I will never return
because I have come home to face this wreckage:
that Joan is my mother.... and Ivan is my father

but if I were a child again, I would tell me
you were born beautiful, holy like light streaming through stained
glass
you have the tools to cut down fear, walk tall
you are a moving masterpiece of stained glass and shark tooth
strength
please know, that you are enough
and you are loved, you are loved, you are loved;
I am loved, I am loved, I am loved
and I am a poet
and I might not have been
but this is how I meet you today

and that makes all the difference

A Letter to the Road I didn't Travel

by
Alicia Payne

Dear road I didn't travel,

How do I put this gently? Stop stalking me!

I've made a decision and I'm sticking to it, thank you very much. To expect me to compare my life without you to what it could have been is oh, so, unfair. I didn't take you. So I really have no idea where you would have taken me.

True, once upon a time I thought I wanted to be a teacher...in the public school system. Road, stop laughing! I know you well enough to know that you're mocking me, or at least chuckling and snorting. Though I have dear friends who are teachers, I also know that, for a while, there was a manufactured crisis, at least in Ontario. Some would say there still is a crisis. The point is, had I taken you, I may have been one of the newbies bounced for lack of seniority. Which means you could have been leading me to a dead end. Who knows? And despite my experience as a teaching assistant, teachers' college didn't want me. Truth be told, thankfully, you're the one who initially rejected me.

Well—and I don't at all consider this cheating—I got there anyway. I took a little side road that led to another and another... Yes, initially you were attractive and potentially stable and reliable and possibly even fun. Not to mention you're a road that many people approved of and even encouraged me towards. And yet, like all roads, there was no guarantee of anything. So I went with the little road that kept beckoning me. It was narrow at first and overhung with branches and other mystery elements that intrigued me. Though I resisted, the artist in me couldn't help exploring it. I tiptoed along for a while. Eventually, I learned and grew. Then I added artist educator to the labels that try to define me. Now I'm invited to teach and work in schools—other places, too! I get to work with kids of all ages, including adults. And I love it!

Just so you know, you're not the only road I considered travelling. Surprised? That's right. You weren't the only road on my list. For a while, I thought law school was the place to be. It, too, rejected me. Years later, I was suddenly thrust into a human rights "project." I loved it less...a lot less. Procedural wrangling and stalling to discourage people from standing up for their rights has never been my style. For a while, my pursuit of justice stifled and sucked the creative energy right out of me. Happily, I remain passionate about human rights. The writer and artist educator in me has had the joy and honor of working on artistic projects that address human rights creatively. That's much more my style.

Paris, I know you're out there. Forgive me for leaving. I had to. Oh la la! Had I stayed, what would have become of me? Je ne sais pas.

Past relationships, each one of you was a trip! I'm not even going there.

So many roads, so many travels. To be honest, from time to time, I wonder what my life would be like had I taken any one of you. How many of the people I cherish in my life would still be here in my heart? Of those who have passed, would they have been in my life? And what of the friends I've lost contact with and the would-have-been friends I never met?

I don't know. And it no longer matters. I have chosen a path that at times feels like it has chosen me. I'm sure I've missed and misinterpreted signs along the way. It goes with the territory. I'm not turning back. (Not that time would let me).

Ultimately, by choosing the path I'm on, I found and am finding myself, my life, my work, family, friends and play. Everything that is, was, and is about to become a part of me has been rerouted by choice. The choices *I* made. The roads I didn't travel and the roads I have taken. Despite the unexpected and sometimes excruciatingly difficult twists and turns along the way, my journey has also come with joy and blessings.

So, Road. Roads I didn't travel, time has passed. You're not the same road. I'm definitely not the same person. I'm happy here in this moment. No matter how many times you try to get me to revisit you, I can't. I won't.

Thank you for what I learned. Thank you for what I avoided.

Now excuse me. My chosen path continues to call and I choose to answer.
I wish you and those on your path safe and wondrous travels.

With love and appreciation,

Alicia

SEASON 4: PART TWO

A LETTER TO MY GRANDMOTHER
January 18, 2015

Louise Boltbee

Elizabeth Cinello

Stacy Gardner

Helen Picard

Shelly Sanders

Samantha Vakiener

A Letter to My Grandmother

by
Louise Boltbee

Dear Gram:

My mind has decided to join the circus again today. Right now it's auditioning, simultaneously I might add, for every high wire, tightrope and acrobatic act imaginable. When I feel like this inside, I come to you. I draw you near me just like when I was a child and I wrapped myself in the quilts you made for us. I know you struggled with your own thoughts and in the end you found a measure of peace. This always gives me comfort and makes me think it is possible for me, too.

In this moment, though, I can't tell whether everything is falling apart or falling into place. Hmmmm...yes...maybe it is both. And maybe that makes me much more of a quilter like you than I ever imagined. I really like this thought. Quilts, after all, are made of other things, aren't they? Repurposed fragments, memories, and old usefulnesses—all shadows of their former selves. You know, I remember how Mom would look at one of your quilts and say, "These pieces here came from old flour sacks. I had a dress made out of this one. And the kitchen curtains in Aylmer were made of that one, over there."

But Gram, what do I do when everything that is familiar to me is falling apart at the seams? Costumes, customs, habits, all the weavings of my world are disintegrating, like those old kitchen curtains of yours. My grief for this loss shrieks like winter winds and these winds whip everything up into a frantic blizzard of bits and pieces. I am blinded by my own panic. Where is my normal going?

Well, I don't really care if my normal wasn't balanced or healthy or loving. It was familiar, known and reliable. And that made it comfortable. Wow, hearing myself say these words is really quite revealing, isn't it?

Your hands were always soft and cool even in the heat of summer. And right now I feel as though your hands are resting on my own. "Be still," your touch seems to say, "Let them be. All those fragments – those leftovers – they're simply the foundation of a quilt, little pieces of possibility. Yes, Louise, little pieces of possibility. And if you play with them, create with them, they will continue to deteriorate until they simply dissolve back into pure possibility, taking you with them."

Gram, that's beautiful. You know, I began writing this letter because I was so bent out of shape that I needed to ground myself and because I thought you were gone…dead. I mean, we write letters to those who are away from us, don't we? But you're not gone at all. You are here with and within me and you are so whole. I feel you and you are such a blending of all you have ever been. And there is this quality of youthful ancientness. Yet, you are still growing—though free of any of the ghosts of the mind that haunted you before. You are alive and free.

You're delighted I am able to sense this. I see your beautiful blue eyes looking back at me over the tops of your glasses. Resting within your gaze, ever so slightly mesmerized, it dawns on me that because I can feel this bloom in your being I, too, must be more whole, more free and more alive than I think I am. My immediate and automatic reaction is to file this revealing away as a particularly interesting curiosity in my collection. However, when I move with the usual efficiency to place this beautiful possibility within my inventory, I feel nauseous.

As though to silence yourself, you have gathered your hands and are pressing the two tips of your index fingers to your smiling lips. You so want to share a secret but know you can't spoil the surprise. Whatever it is, I am suddenly aware, it is imperative I figure it out for myself. And with that acknowledgement, you close your eyes. Everything becomes very quiet. All light is extinguished. You have escorted me to a threshold. And now it is up to me to feel my way across.

Sinking more deeply into sensing, I appreciate this is not a threshold that takes me from here to there. Instead, I have to let go. Yes—I know I have to let go. I hesitate not out of fear, I realize, but out of respect. I wish to be fully present in this moment. I catch my breath when I realize it is the act of being present, rather than the letting go, that turns the key in the lock. Release floods me with relief. I cannot move. I do not need to move. So sacred is this surrender.

My willingness initiates an unfolding of action, which reveals itself in a flow of images. There is a beautiful woman dressed in wedding white descending a long, long staircase. I am she. I am leaving the house of my youth, the tower of my mind. Stepping slowly I lovingly luxuriate in all I have ever known of this home. Silently savouring, I look once and for all out through the white-washed ossified windows of the senses.

Sight, sound, smell, and taste look back lovingly and each takes its place gently holding the end of the train of my gown. With each step I take the train extends and descends without end into the deepening darkness. Though I have passed from their view we feel each other, my bridesmaids and I, in the soft folds of the fabric that flows from my waist back to their touch. Without a shadow of doubt the promise of my presence rings clear and true in their waiting hearts.

The steps disappear and red is the path of roses that rises up to greet me. As soft and fragrant as the night these dew-kissed petals dissolve suddenly and silently into a river of redness.

Carrying me, ferrying me endlessly and effortlessly these crimson waters deliver me home to my heart.

Though not necessary, there is a door through which I may enter. It is a beautiful gift from my beloved who wishes to honour me with the pleasure of savouring all the subtleties of my own homecoming. I summon the winds—all four of them. Washing me in their whispers they gently gather and lift my veil so I may see my mirror clearly and say silently, "All is One. Love melt the something of me into the everything of us."

And with those words a fire, the likes of which Hell could only dream of, ignites itself. Leaping to life from within this open and whole heart of ours it gathers everything into the folds of its flames. And, as promised, a barrage of friendly fire is dispatched to burn back up the trail of my train and swallow into our seamlessness that myriad maze of steps, my bridesmaids together with all their senses and that tower of the mind. Though looking more like a little attic, that tower will forever be a treasure to me for it was within its walls I learned my humanity is the key to my divinity.

Oh, Gram...how right you are. What a beautiful unending surprise to watch all those pieces of possibility eternally fashioning themselves into the peace of all possibility. I shall be quilting forever and a day.

Thank you, love you,

Louise.

A Letter to My Grandmother

by
Elizabeth Cinello

Chère Mémère,

I'll start by saying I never order gnocchi or ravioli in a restaurant. Too soft or too hard, these *primi* are always a disappointment. Overcooked and underwhelming is how I describe my friends' gnocchi and ravioli. Between you and me, I eat to be polite. No one can top your cooking. That's because my mother crams your homemade pasta recipes with lots of flavour – stories about you and her childhood in France, during WWII. When the mood strikes her, she calls me up and says, "Let's make gnocchi." The recipe is a hot trigger. Memories ooze. "It was our job, the four youngest kids, to line up the gnocchi in neat straight lines," she says. "It kept us calm and focused."

We never skip your quirky recipe step – the gnocchi grid. Just like you taught my mother when she was a kid, she taught me to evenly space the gnocchi so that they don't touch and stick together. They're so delicate. I handle them gently, careful not to squish them with impatient fingers. *Voilà.* I place them on the kitchen counter near the stove, on a lightly floured white cotton cloth, where they wait patiently and good-naturedly, *bien arrangés*, for their destiny – the pot of boiling water.

By my teens, I mastered all the steps. Boil, cool, peel, and rice the potatoes; add flour, make dough, let it rest. Roll pieces of dough into meter-long logs, pinch and cut gnocchi-sized cubes; roll each *gnocco* off the back of a fork. My mother says the older kids were in charge of that step and you had a special fork for the job. I know the tines leave crevices for the sauce to latch on to but we don't do it. My mother says it's a waste of time. Next, set up the gnocchi grid. Toss the gnocchi into a pot of boiling salted water; scoop them up when they float to the top, place

125

them on a serving dish, add sauce. Repeat in batches. Keep them warm over a *bain-marie* set-up until you're ready to eat. *Mémère*, you were a crafty chef. You transformed the compliant potato into a gourmet stomach-stuffing meal while training your nine hungry kids to be obedient line chefs.

I've missed a step in your recipe, one that we take for granted today. You had to get the potatoes. My mother's stories of tracking down food and bringing it from farm to table, during the war, play out like grim fairytale quests where the treasure is not a pot of gold or a magic ring, but something to eat, like a basket of blue-skinned plums, a dozen golden eggs, a head of cabbage. Did things happen the way she remembers them? It doesn't matter, but I am curious because when I think of French cuisine I think of you and the family, in Hayange, near the French/German border, scrounging for food. The story of the *tête de chou* (head of cabbage), Alsace-Lorraine's prized vegetable, stands out. Do you remember it?

My mother would have been eight years old, maybe nine. *Grand-père* was hiding in the hills between Hayange and Knutange. The Germans were looking for him. My mother was sharp and fast on her feet. Her task was to bring him lunch and run errands for him. She was the go-between. No one would suspect a little girl. What would have happened if someone had noticed her?

Every now and then, *grand-père* gave her a package wrapped in heavy brown paper, held together by a tightly wound string that finished off in a little bow. You told her to take the package to Madame Maria. Like you and *grand-père*, Madame Maria was a second generation Franco-Italian. She ran a rooming house and an adjacent restaurant requisitioned by the German army for officers who were stationed in Hayange. Their orders were to hunt down and arrest subversives and other enemies of the state, and transfer prisoners across the border to Germany.

Madame Maria had a cabbage patch behind her rooming house and a rare large garden to grow potatoes. "Madame will give you a head of cabbage in exchange for the package," you told my mother. This was very important. The countryside was blown up and fresh produce was hard to find. You warned my mother, "*Attention*, don't leave the package unless Madame

Maria gives you *la tête de chou*." My mother was to bring the cabbage straight home. Do you remember?

Doggedly, she delivered the package to Madame Maria who took it, thanked her, and gave her the cabbage, "*Merci beaucoup ma petite et salut à ta mère.*"

"I was curious," my mother says. "The package was neatly wrapped and it looked like a present. One day, I opened it." She says the thing inside the parcel had a heavy dense weight to it. What could be worth a fine head of cabbage she wondered as she pulled the string from the bow, loosening the wrapping paper, and revealing its contents – a hairy animal with stumpy legs, a long thin tail, a pointed muzzle, elongated teeth, and whiskers. It stared up at her with a scowl. It was dead.

"Right away, I regretted it. I was confused." She quickly rewrapped the thing and tightened the string around it. Faster than ever, she ran to Madame's rooming house.

"Madame Maria looked at the parcel. I had wrapped it quickly, badly. She eyed it. She eyed me.
'You opened it didn't you?'
'Oui, Madame,' I admitted it. It was obvious. Madame glanced down at the package.
'Don't think we eat it ourselves,' she said, 'We don't. We cook it and feed it to the German
officers.'"

My mother's hands grasp an imaginary cabbage head the size of a soccer ball. "Madame gave me *une belle tête de chou.* I ran home holding it in my arms, trying not to drop it."

Back in your kitchen, *mémère*, you went to work on the cabbage head. My mother watched you trim its outer leaves and plop it whole into a pot of boiling water. Then, you julienned the vegetable, which was cooked *al dente*, tossed it with oil and vinegar, and seasoned it with salt, pepper, and juniper berries. The pot of water, infused with the cabbage head's sweetness, made a tasty rice soup for the family. *Bonne Appétit.* In Madame's capable hands, the thing in the package became the main ingredient in a flavourful bourguignon stew, as only the French can make. *Guten Appetit.*

My mother remembers that you, your sisters, and your parents, laughed when she told you what she had found in the parcel. *Mémère*, what if German intelligence had zeroed in on my mother at Madame's kitchen door? Would the cabbage have been worth it? I'd rather not think about it. Did you? Did Madame? What about *grand-père*, wasn't he worried?

Sometimes, the girl who delivered the officers' deliciously gruesome dinner steps forward. Wars and bombings in faraway places grab her attention. She imagines that children and their families are starving. Before she retired, she worked at a wholesaler in the city's west end where she arranged a food drive for St. Francis Table on Queen Street. Every month, she loaded up her car and delivered the healthy food to the good brothers.

You'll be pleased to know that my mother has an appetite for the good things in life, for the quietly patient gnocchi that taste so good. I thank you for that. When she cooks she considers every ingredient and its qualities. She mines the city for the sweetest grapes, the creamiest camembert, the crunchiest fennel.

The *tête de chou* is still a part of my mother's cuisine: baked cabbage rolls stuffed with *risotto* and dressed with tomato sauce; sautéed cabbage and onion with white wine; red cabbage cooked with apple. Once in a while, *choucroute* (sauerkraut) finds its way to the table, cuddled up against a fat sausage.

I just remembered, when we were young, she would call us *mon petit chou* or *mon chouchou* (my little cabbage, my sweetie). "I'm not your shoe," we would answer back, and she would laugh.
Salut chère Mémère. Ta petite fille, your granddaughter,

Elizabeth

P.S. What did you barter for the potatoes?

A Letter to My Grandmother

by
Stacy Gardner

Dear Nan,

I'm wearing slippers knit by you, and just tucked Cohen into bed under one of your quilts. It was good to see you yesterday. I am so glad you are here for us to know, to have.

At 91-years-old, your hair, frothy and white, your memory intact, your wit still shocking, and your fretful sorrow for things lost, as always, an insufferable salt that has sifted and settled into your bones, *less*, your cove. Your soul, still sailing, wailing, *Why Not Me?*

I didn't know *exactly* what I was asking you when I was only nine-years-old, *buoyant* like one of your golden retrievers for the bread you'd bake every Sunday night. It was dessert after our supper. You'd take four to six loaves out of the oven, and place them each on the counter like newborns, soft, malleable, each awaiting your massage of butter, their heat, softening the wax paper that pampered each one. You'd put one aside to cut, and cloak the others under the cape of a small linen tablecloth.

Did you have dreams Nan? It seemed as natural to ask as, *Can I have another slice of bread, Nan?*

You obliged, accompanied my thick buttery slice with a mug of Tetley Tea, which I used for more dipping than sipping, and ignored my question.

Well? I reminded, through chirps and slurps.

I don't remember which sister kicked me in the shin under the table. She was surely older. But you kept your back to me when you replied with a sniffled huff, *What kind of foolish question is that now?*

It didn't seem foolish. You were to me then, only as I knew, My Grandmother, and that of twenty other bread-lovin' grandkids, too. My Father's Mother. Mother of four boys and two girls. Wife of Lloyd. Or as you pronounced, *Lied*. He called you *Bet*, short for Elizabeth. And we called you both Nanny and Pappy.

I've come to know that, "*Don't be so foolish*" in Newfoundland is cousin of, "*Whaddya wanna know that for?*" or "*No one wants to hear that sure.*" Which means it's an easy place to become a troublemaker, an outsider, *or*, one that is too accommodating.

Remember when I was about six or seven, and I flicked myself through the screen door of your summer house by the sea with flowers *for you*? I loved that place. You called it a cabin, but it was a four-bedroom harbour, nestled between mountains and ocean, made warm even in winter. You would knit by the woodstove, watching *All My Children* passively on the television, getting up every once in a while to check on dinner. Pappy, somewhere nearby, reading or rebuilding or making his own fishing flies.

It's gone now, that house and wharf. All ravaged and washed away by the reckless disregard of weather and family. Pappy's Death. The wharf. The one he built, and then built again with his sons over time. The one I was always weary of venturing upon, despite its sturdy build and fine intricacies. Where I used to crouch and sing to all the snails in shells that clung to its wet posts, with the most horrifying of lyrics! Though, when sung in the sweetest shade, without fail, they always magically worked:
Snail, Snail, come out of your house,
or I will kill your mother and father.

And it would slowly appear, and I would be instantly enchanted.

You had such a fright on your face when I entered the kitchen with my varied bouquet. You softly shouted: *Where'd you get those flowers to?*

On the mountain, I replied.

It was a vertical and vast land mass about 30 feet high behind your house; steep, but soft enough to scramble up, and severe enough to tumble down in a hurry. It had a bountiful meadow at its top, and lots of flowers brought on by summer.

Or so I thought.

That frantic shame of worry on your face began to ripple, and bogged down with insistence and reluctance, you asked me again:

Yes, but where on the mountain did you get those flowers, m'love?—adding "my love" for just the right amount of comfort.

Still spirited from my discovery, I simply replied, *Where all the trophies are, Nan, some have flowers, some don't.*

Oh My Jesus! you said. *Do you remember the names?*

Just a couple, Nan, I didn't read 'em all, there was too many...Mr. Tucker. Mrs. Fisher. Mrs. Sheppard.

Oh My, you huffed, *Sure Mrs. Sheppard was only buried last week.* And then, *Did anybody see you?*

I shrugged, you found a vase and then explained to me what a graveyard was.

Dreams, you tut in response more than 30 years later. Your mind all-knowing, your body, nowhere as reliable. You sit in a home that is yours, for now, finally a room available after almost six months in hospital waiting for one. The fall you caught, finally the one that took you from yours, permanently.

'Dat oil must be curdling already, you mocked, *t'is still some 'ting awful when you've got to wait 'dat long for your own bed.*

I echo your distrust of a corrupt and reactive government, the feigned wealth and its unfair distribution, and pour you a cup of Tetley.

You add to it, telling me of the time, how Pappy told off Brian Tobin, who was out *'gallivantin' around on his boat with friends, and mistook Pappy's Wharf, for The Governor's Wharf',* which was only a few drafts of wind west, and he said: *Do you like the wharf we gave you, Mr. Gardner?*

Pappy shook his fist in the air, and spat: *You Bastard, you've given me nothing! I built this wharf, and everything else you see.*

He was a good man, your Pappy, did you like him? You asked.

Of course, I laughed. And then: *Did you?*

I loved him, you said.

Now as an adult, I find it a source of amazement that my Grandfather made a good life from self-made mercantile interests, and was retired for more than 40 years when he died in his eighties. On the night he had died, it was only hours before that he was out fixing the door on another one of his cabins, and pulling potatoes from the earth.

Enough about Pappy, I say, passing you a Werthers' candy.

Oh my love, you moan, *sure, what do you want me to say? Me father took me out of school when I was 13 to take care of the family.*

Your heartbreak, ever-present, as you dab tears made up of more than 80 years of swell and squall.

He was some strict, you pressed.

I know the word strict. It's a tidier version of a harsher crime and time. But you don't go there.

Even on Sundays when I was havin' a little play for meself, when the sun was hot, and the days were long, I had to come home early, and take care of me boys. My brothers, you correct.

Of course, it would make sense to think of your brothers, your own children. The youngest was only two-years-old when your mother died, the year you were 13 and made mother of a household and seven brothers.

All of those boys me father put through university, except for me.

You weep and wipe, and I take your hand.

The wound of having no childhood, girlhood, or education, thrashes against the shoreline more certainly than acknowledging the pain of having lost your Dear Mother Louise in childbirth.

Had she lived, would you have more than survived?

You don't know. You don't even like to be angry at anyone. But you feel it. It's yours. And you belong to it as much. Shackled by a disappointment that despite having your own family, and a hearty life with Pappy, you never knew the course you *might* have been able to chart, or which anchor you *might* have rested *your* laurels upon.

But you did do good, Nan.

It's hard for you to believe. You always think that when I want to know something, or understand it better, that I am trying to poke holes in your world, and make you look *foolish.*

Would I have survived so well in the time you had lived on such a tragic island?

I remind you that I cannot sew, neither stitch nor button. Cannot cook without using measuring cup and recipe book. Fretful of the fact that I can't just knit something for a friend. Nor do I have the nerve to jig a cod for fun or for dinner, or a mathematical mind and foresight to play a game of Crib against You.

You, who peered through the bedroom door and watched the doctor lay your dead baby brother against your dead mother, you saw all the blood, and you wiped your tears and did what needed to be done.

Your Resilience, Humour and Strength, are sturdier than any wharf built by any man.

Love, Stacy

132

A Letter to My Grandmother

by
Helen Picard

ABCs

This is a letter to you, grandma, because I could not speak or write when you were sixty, and you could not write or speak when you were seventy. Time gave me fluency of speech and a legible hand, but eroded yours in a way neither of us could understand. Because telomeres and tissue loss, neurofibrillary tangles and twisted fibres are not on the primary or elementary school syllabi. I learned my ABC's while yours were tangled and taken from you — C for cell death, B for beta amyloid, A for Alzheimer's.

You were a schoolteacher and a mother, in both Montreal and Toronto, so you knew your ABC's, and taught them to others; but not these. On the first cool day of autumn in 1994 you took me for a carriage ride, and we got lost, you and I. A suburban labyrinth of pavement and trees swallowed us. C for carriage. Some helpful neighbours called my parents, who picked us up. That must have been the last we spent time alone together.

From then on, you were a Christmas visit before going to my Aunt's house for macaroni salad, ham, and presents. Grandma's sick, that's what they told me. The vacancy in your eyes scared me, but you still looked gentle and kind: remnants of your personality and the beautiful life you led. But still, every visit was the same — I played on the carpet with my sister and cousins while the adults talked, and you seemed to listen from your wheelchair. C is not for eye contact. Nor is it for conversation. The only memory I have of you talking is when, long after I learned my ABC's, you pointed to the framed picture of me on the coffee table, then a lanky ten-year old with glasses, and said, "baby." If C if for carriage, B is for Baby. A, of course, is for Alzheimer's.

This letter is for you, grandma, because our fates are as uncertain and intertwined as our walk that cool autumn day. This letter is for you grandma, because it is also for me; because A is the start and end, like an old woman pushing a baby in a stroller. Both are lost, and both are at the start of something. Neither is fully formed, and both are uncertain. Both are simply uncertain in the most complicated ways. A for Alzheimer's, B for beta amyloid, C for cell death. And I wish it could stop there, but it goes on: D is for dementia, E is for early onset, F is for family, and G is for genetics.

Which is why, grandma, our ABCs are so simple, yet so complex. And an old woman pushing a baby in a stroller is not just through a labyrinth of trees, but of neural endings: roots, branches, leaves, rippling electrically in the baby's realization, twenty years later, that she is still there with the old woman, searching in vain for a way out of their own entanglement, which is shared, and inevitable, and young, and old.

This letter is for you, grandma, because my thoughts are straight now, like broad avenues, but may later be marked by peculiar consistencies: identical lampposts lining an endless street, glowing with importance and significance, but without understanding. Their draw cannot be extinguished, because I know they are important, but cannot recall why. I am following them, towing this inkling, this infant suspicion that there's some turn I missed, that I've lost myself in this labyrinth of streets and trees that wave at me, in on the secret. This letter is for you, grandma, because these ABCs, these letters, this letter, was, is, and will be ours.

A Letter to My Grandmother

by
Shelly Sanders

Dear Nana,

Every time I speak about the books I've written, inspired by your life, I'm inevitably asked the following question: "What would your grandmother think about you exposing her past?" I have no way of knowing because you died when I was just twelve. So my response varies and is not rooted in fact. Basically, I lie and tell people I'm sure you would be pleased knowing that your secret is out. But the truth is, as your namesake, I feel kind of guilty, and am worried that you might actually be annoyed with me. After all, you hid your past from your own daughter (my mother) until she found out, by accident at twenty-four.

You were so determined to conceal your roots that you managed to sheath yourself in a new persona when you came to Canada, a façade you never removed. But beneath the surface, I can't help but wonder if you ever secretly wanted to return to the culture that formed you, to the traditions that led to your frightening exodus.

While I can't take back what I've written, especially in this era of social media, where rumors spread through cyberspace's tentacles faster than a disease, I can explain why I ended up divulging your carefully guarded secret. Blame your sister, Nucia. It all started with her in Montreal on a hot summer afternoon six months after my first child, Amanda, was born. It was a battle of wills, me plying her with questions and she doing her best to evade them. Luckily, Nucia was no match against my shrewd reporter skills. After assuring her that I would keep any information she gave me within the family (a white lie that was necessary, if

135

not ethical) she began telling me about your shared childhood in Russia, your escape to Shanghai and your illicit relationship with the man who would become my grandfather. My hand shook as I listened and wrote, finally getting the long-awaited glimpse into your world, how you lived, and the perils you faced because of your religion. I was especially moved by your courage which helped guide you to California where you received a Commerce degree from the University of California at Berkeley in 1930.

Nucia's information formed the plot of your life, why you went from one place to another. But it didn't reveal who you were and made me wish I'd been older when you died, mature enough to care about my heritage, curious enough to ask questions that went beyond, "Did you bring me a souvenir from Barbados?"

I look at photos of you as a young woman, hair in a thick braid that falls to your waist, your unreadable eyes, and wonder what you were doing when told you had to abandon your house one night. What important things were you forced to leave behind when the pogrom erupted, with houses set on fire? What were you thinking as you fled east, across Russia, and took a boat to Shanghai which accepted you without papers, without questions, without prejudice? When I heard this, I realized I owe my existence to Shanghai. Your aunts and uncles who weren't able to leave Russia, perished in the revolution, and those who sought refuge in Europe, died in the Holocaust.

What shook me most was hearing Nucia say that I was considered Jewish, because you were my maternal grandmother. She told me that if I'd lived in Europe during World War II, I'd have been forced to wear the Yellow Star of David, and would have been sent to a death camp. This revelation hit me hard. Discovering the fact that I would be accepted as Jewish, like you, made me feel connected to you. For the first time, I understood why you'd kept your faith a secret, but I was no closer to knowing how you'd feel about me blowing your cover.

By the end of my afternoon with Nucia, you'd become my hero, and I had a newfound appreciation for my roots. I tried to put myself in your shoes, wondering how you coped under an

136

anti-Semitic authoritarian ruler. I wanted to know what you talked about, what you ate, what you wore, what you did for fun. What you dreamed about. What frightened you.

I began researching Russian pogroms; hundreds took place in shetls all over Russia. How did you function, knowing you could be attacked at any time? I discovered that Jews in Russia who converted to Christianity would no longer be considered Jewish and, therefore, were no longer targets during pogroms. Your family chose to keep its faith and leave Russia, which implied a steadfast desire to hold onto Judaism. Yet you ended up marrying a Christian and forsaking your own religion. Were you tired of running, of living in fear? Did love trump faith?

When I stumbled upon the 1903 Kishinev pogrom, ignited by vicious and fraudulent newspaper headlines, I knew at once that I had to write about it. As a journalist myself, the idea that a publisher would spread propaganda through his newspaper, abusing his power, disturbed and enthralled me. The glimmer of a book began to percolate in my mind. And when I discovered a Kishinev family with two children, who suffered unjustly from this horrific event, I decided to name the children Rachel and Nucia, to honor you and your sister. My character Rachel took on your traits—curiosity, intelligence, a strong-will. Wanting more from life than was expected at the time. I started living vicariously through you as I wrote, trying to get inside your head, to think like you'd think, to feel like you'd feel. In this way, I got to know you better and felt closer than ever. It was a life-changing experience for me and I hope you'll forgive any liberties I took.

The settings for all three books mirror your journey to freedom, but fiction diverges with history. My character arrives in California in late 1905, 22 years before you, and just in time for the 1906 San Francisco earthquake which displaced the immigrant community. Plus, she has to learn English in America whereas you learned the language in Shanghai. It takes her years to graduate from high school while you landed and went straight to Berkeley.

Both you and Rachel get into university, and both of you struggle with your faith; the character Rachel must figure out how to balance her dream of being an American with her old-fashioned traditions. You gave up your Judaism entirely when you

137

settled in Montreal where signs proclaimed, "No blacks, no dogs, no Jews." Nobody, me included, could ever judge you for ever making this choice, especially when, on the eve of the second World War, Canada turned boatloads of European Jews away, Jews who ended up perishing in death camps. Still, I've been told that although you raised your girls in the Anglican faith of my grandfather, you never spoke during a church service, never sang a hymn, took communion, or recited from the Bible. To me, this means you might have harbored a lifetime affinity for Judaism, tucked safely in your heart where nobody could see it.

I finally found the answer I'd been searching for while listening to an orphaned Holocaust survivor. He said that his seven grandchildren and the continuation of his Jewish heritage are the prizes he received from the war Hitler lost. And he said he speaks now in honor of his parents, who don't have a grave, telling their story so that they didn't perish for nothing. Addressing the youth in the audience, he said the people most at fault were those who did nothing. At that moment, I knew I had done the right thing in uncovering your Jewish faith, that I'd told a story that had to be told.

Exposing your past has given me the chance to know and understand you and Russia. I keep photos of you on my desk which remind me daily of my heritage. My favorite is one where you're sitting, holding me as a baby in your lap. Your hands cradle me tight and both of my hands rest on yours, as if I'm embracing you, too.

Writing has allowed me to share you with my children, who I hope will continue to pass these stories along to their children one day, strengthening the ties from generation to generation. For this reason, I am now quite comfortable saying that you would be proud of me and of what I've accomplished, just as I'm proud and honored to have had you as my nana.

A Letter to My Grandmother

by
Samantha Vakiener

I'm just curious.

Are you cool with it all?

I mean, you have three children and they've had seven marriages between them. Not to each other, but...you know what I mean.

It's all still something that's hard for me to wrap my head around.

Your kids' first round of marriages happened before I existed—that is, breathing-wise or memory-wise.

That's why I'm asking you. You're old. You were there. And I'm not apologizing for that. You're my grandmother. You are old.

I've got questions.

How long were they all married for?

Sue to Beau?

Mom to Mark?

David to...I don't know...Diane? Or whoever...

It couldn't have been *that* long.

Mom married Dad when she was 28. No, that's not right. They had Charlie when she was 28, so before that. And she wasn't ever a teenage bride either. Sometime between college and when she was 28, Mom had an entire series of wedding – marriage – divorce...

But let's go back and start with Sue. She's the oldest anyway. And Sue's Beau is the one I know the most about. After college, she broke off her engagement to another guy and took that guy's dog so she could go be with Beau. Beau was older and had diabetes. They got married, but he couldn't have kids, so he said they had to get divorced—saying it wasn't fair to her. She was heartbroken. He remarried, adopted an Asian kid and died. So it was a medical reason? "It" being the cause of divorce.

Was hers the first of your kids' weddings? The first divorce? What did you say? Did you skip the fuss in hope of grandkids?

What was the deal with David's first wife? I can only assume David divorced...Donna? Dina? Because of the one time they babysat Charlie and she sat on his teddy, Thurmond, the entire time, so Charlie wailed and wailed and she just sat there, not thinking to remedy the situation in any fashion. That's the only thing I've ever heard about her so that must be the reason.

The first I ever heard of Mom having a first husband was in the middle of middle school, and I've only heard Mark mentioned a handful of times since. Had my dad really been roommates or frat brothers or something with the guy in college? I've gathered Mark and Mom had their problems, but did my dad steal her away on top of all of that? What did you think when my mom said she was marrying my dad?

This is coming out of the blue...I've never asked about these people before. The info I have is all gleaned from snippets overheard from you guys during years of cocktail hours. You all mention them in front of me, but it's never like I've partook in the conversations. I guess I'm allowed to know, but am I allowed to ask? Part of me has wanted to dig.

What has gone on in all your lives before me?

I'm asking you because, to ask my mom would be too weird. I heard enough about divorce from her when I was seventeen and she split with my dad, swore never to marry again and then did a few years later. Her new husband, he's fine. But he's her third. And not my dad.

Three.

You grew up in a time when getting divorced was a major taboo. What did you do the moment each of your kids broke the news? Now they feel like moments swept under the rug.

You're still married to Papa. After all these years...You ever think you might have gotten a divorce if it hadn't been such a societal no-no? Did you staying married affect your kids' thoughts on marriage?

I guess what I'm getting at is what do you think of the fate of marriages?

"Till death do us part" only seems to work for your kids' generation the second or third time around.

I've found a man whom I plan to marry someday. It would be a first marriage for us both.

Do we have a chance?

I think we do. Like how my mom's generation moved away from the norms of yours, mine is finding it's own way too.

Today, we find our loves on the Internet. Don't worry. I'm not going to attempt to tune you in on the workings of technology here. That's a discussion for another day.

All I'm saying is, I think my peers have a leg up over earlier generations' chances at finding lasting love. I was able to screen out the crazies before hand-selecting a man with good tastes, looks, and ideals according to me. We got through the, "Do you have any siblings?" "What kind of music do you like?" and "You're not into hard drugs or anything?" small talk before ever meeting face to face. With all that out of the way, we were free to let ourselves fall for each other without worrying what small disagreement could blow up into a major tear in our relationship down the line.

You will meet him someday soon – I hope you like him – I'm keeping him around for a very long time.

SEASON 4: PART THREE

A LETTER TO MY 18-YEAR-OLD SELF
April 12, 2015

Ann Eyerman

Lauren Gillies

Tanya Neumeyer

Dryden Rainbow

A Letter to My 18-Year-Old Self

by
Ann Eyerman

Dear Annie Eyerman,

Oh my goodness, it's nice to see you. I'm looking at that picture of you sitting in that sweet yellow-and-white-gingham dress that Susie had made for herself. You certainly were fortunate to have generous sisters who shared their clothes with you and who had a lot better taste than you did. Oh, you were so shy when that guy came into the office on that Saturday morning. He said he was from the university paper, *The Lantern*, and wanted to take your picture. Did you blush a little? I think you did. But I think you were also a little scared of him. Was it because there was no one else around, or because he was *flirting* with you? I think the latter. Did you even know how to recognize flirting? Probably not. It's really too bad, that you hadn't had a lot more experience with flirting and dating and necking and crushes and broken hearts during high school. It would have made your life a whole lot more fun and not so heartbreaking when you started working at the university. But you didn't. And that was that!

You gave the guy with the camera one of your flip, (what Mom would have called) smart-alecky, replies. It was your defense. You just couldn't believe that some nice, young guy with a camera would really think you were cute enough to take a picture of. But you sure were. Yet, even though you told him his camera was going to break if he took a picture of *you*, you still let him do it. I liked that a lot about your spirit. You cocked your head back and laughed when he put the camera to his eye and ordered you to say, "Go Buckeyes." But then you didn't even ask him what his name was or what he was studying. Normal, "girl-meets-boy-on-college-campus," kind of talk. You let him leave before he could ask you go to out on a date or have a Coke or walk down by Mirror Lake that summer afternoon. But I understand because you just didn't know how to have those kinds of conversations, did you?

And why should you have? You went through those awful four years at St. Francis de Sales High School where you might as well have been invisible for all any of those boys ever noticed. Did anyone ever say, "Hi Ann, want to go to the sock hop?" Or, at the sock-hop, come over and ask you to dance a slow dance? Not a one—oh, wait a minute, there was Frankie Freemont who came over and said, "Well, there's no one else to ask so I might as well dance with you." Not exactly confidence-building material when it comes to boys and flirting and feeling good about yourself.

But, you know what, Annie, even if you didn't have a lot of confidence in yourself or your looks or your smarts or anything else, you still had a lot of spunk. There you were, your little 18-year-old, naive, poorly educated, wrong-side-of-Cleveland-Avenue self bunged smack down in the middle of all those over-educated, egotistical, French-speaking, older academics, and you didn't drown or run away or go mute or quit. Bravo, girl, bravo, bravo.

It wasn't easy, though, was it? You constantly had to be on High Alert when they came into that big open room to get their mail. You didn't have any place to hide, no door to close, no shelter from their storm. You, Annie Eyerman, were an open target for anything they wanted to throw your way, whether some sharp, clever quip or a question they knew you couldn't answer, or just totally ignoring you like you weren't sitting right there in front of them. How did you ever get any work done at all?

I know, most of the time you didn't have a clue what those guys were talking about anyway. That's why you got to be real, real good at listening, observing and honing those little sarcastic barbs of yours so you could hide your ignorance from them and hope they didn't see through it. That was hard work, my friend.

But the real sad part is that the better you got at the banter and the longer you sat at that old wooden desk, the easier it was to forget that you were *just* 18 years-old, Annie. You were still a girl, not a woman. 18—not 22 or 25 or 30 like the guys you went out to lunch with every day at Pomerean Hall. You thought they took you and Susie along because they liked your company, and they probably did. Why wouldn't they? You two weren't like the graduate students they were dating. You were pure. Not in the sense of your virginity, regarding which you certainly were pure-pure-pure, but that you were fresh, naive, sweet, *pliable*. And because of that, they tried to change who you were. Remember when you got all excited at lunch because you were going to the football game on Saturday? You were chattering on about your favorite players and how you loved the marching band and how just being in the stadium was so great. Then one of them said in that, "I am older and definitely wiser" voice: "Annie, there are big things and small things and Ohio State sports is **not** a big thing." It made you sad and embarrassed didn't it?

So after that, you tried to hide that 18-year-old self deeper inside. But that got harder for you when they started asking you out on real dates. It was one thing being their lunch mascot but another sitting in a dark movie theater and not knowing what to do about that arm around your shoulders.

Oh, sweet Annie, you were caught somewhere in-between being a girl and being a woman and not comfortable in either place. You were good with your womanly disguise. You had older sisters who were already "out there in the world" working and dating and going to movies and dances at the Valley Dale on Saturday nights. You picked up clues from them and borrowed their grown-up dresses and high-heeled shoes. But that was only your facade. Inside, your heart was still full of swooning, teen-aged, put-your-head-on-my-shoulder dreams of romance. It wasn't easy was it Annie?

147

Oh, it's too bad that your first falling-in-love wasn't with someone else other than Ned. Like maybe that nice 20-year-old student who took you out to a bar where they played country western music and you drank beers from long-necked bottles and where you understood everything the guy was talking about and didn't have to pretend one time. But that's not how it played out for you. You wore that beating heart of yours on your sleeve for Ned a very, very long time but, it did finally slip off one day and you were free.

You, Annie, were a pretty remarkable 18-year-old. Maybe that's truly what all those guys saw but couldn't appreciate without changing you. I am so thankful to you for somehow holding on to who you were through it all. You know, well you don't, but I'm going to tell you, everything good that got you through the rest of your life you started then. You started to trust that you were intelligent. You started to write and, somewhere deep inside, believed it when people said, "You are a good writer." You started honing your good, albeit sometimes sarcastic, sense of humor. And, you started to love yourself. And even though you hid it so deep in your heart where it couldn't be stolen, it was still there and ready for excavation when the time was right. Thank you again for my life.

With much affection,

Ann

A Letter to My 18-Year-Old Self

by
Lauren Gillies

My Dearest Lauren,

You feel so long ago, but I will never forget you. I still envision you lying broken on our bed; running for hours in the dark, long after our family had gone to sleep; trembling on the bathroom floor wondering when it would all be over. There are times when I search for pictures of you at your worst. I will not deny that I fear you. I fear spiraling downwards into a place where I will once again be completely and utterly debilitated by disorder. When I do catch those remnants of you within me, I feel helpless. I feel haunted by the memories of pure anxiety when you were unable to purge yourself of any nourishment you had consumed. Food was the enemy, not the eating disorder. Anorexia felt like a best friend, a blanket of comfort to turn to when you felt lonely. The less you ate, the more you would become. That's what you believed. I remember wishing that one day we would step onto the scale and see the number zero. Zero pounds, zero failures, zero pain. You could vanish forever; our emaciated body would disappear into the air. Float up, up, up into the sky and never touch back down onto earth. That was what you believed to be real happiness. You remind me of a time in my life that I never want to return to. I feel vulnerable when I relapse. A prisoner, held captive by her own mind. Yet, I can't help but feel drawn to these sentiments. I wish I could tell you that that we break free from our binding thoughts and feelings, that we scare the demons out of our heads. I wish I could tell you that, but I never got better, I just became stronger.

From time to time, I notice remnants of you that are still a part of me. A broken smile, a forced laugh, a flicker of pain in the eyes. The remnants are there. I wish I could tell you that recovery has been easy. That it was but a brief period of our life that has led to bigger and better things. That one morning I sprung out of bed and no longer felt burdened by the suffering we have endured. But this has never been the case. Nothing about recovery has felt painless; every day has been one uphill battle after the next. At one point I truly believed that we had recovered, that we had been able to put the pain in the past. But the truth is, I have yet to learn how to let go.

I cannot ignore the freedom you felt when you arrived at university. You thought that you had left the skeletons at home. A new city would mean a new start. You were wrong. In denying the problems that we are burdened with, we feed them, and they grow stronger until they have the power to consume us.

I still struggle with the emptiness that the pills inflict upon me. I feel humiliated to admit that I do miss the overwhelming sorrow that depression crippled me with. Feeling a sense of total hopelessness and a lack of self-purpose comforted me. It gave me something to hide behind. It scared me to feel nothing at all; I began to think that I would rather endure this eternal sadness than the nothingness the pills brought. I wanted to be taken off the pills, I hated the way that they made me feel, as if they stripped me naked of my emotions and turned me into something of even less value than I already was. I made the decision to stop the Prozac. My emotions and irrational thoughts consumed me once again and I felt out of control. Instead of seeking out help from those around me, I fell back into the habit of restricting my food intake, eating virtually nothing for months, or purging when I consumed any amount of food. I felt like the only place I could feel safe was within the wrath of anorexia and depression. I isolated myself and felt a sense of self-pride that would sicken the average person. I felt powerful and unstoppable, but my thoughts clouded my rational state of being, and I did not notice that my body had begun to deteriorate. I developed atrial tachycardia, a heart arrhythmia, and problems with my digestive tract. I did not reach the point of destruction that you had, but I was getting closer and closer. I was broken and scared, but even more scared of reaching out for help. Somehow I managed to disclose my failure to a therapist. This will forever be the worst part of recovery. Laying bare our demons and problems still feels humiliating. It leaves you feeling naked, but the traits that I valued most about myself were those that were destructing my mind, body, and soul.

Two years after my relapse, I will confess that I still struggle on a day-to-day basis. But I know that I will never again become what I was. Sometimes I feel nervous to run my hands over my hips and no longer feel my bones protruding. It is hard, but I am working to ignore the voices telling me to put down my fork. Right now, this is the first time in my life that I have no plan. I have let go of my careful calculations. It scares me, but somehow, I feel freer.

I am no longer embarrassed of my past. I do not find it shameful to admit that I am a sufferer of mental illness. I no longer feel the need to conceal the darkest parts of myself from people. They're too real to suppress. I no longer feel lonely. The hiding causes that. I wish I could have told you. The hiding, and the sneaking, and the lying only cheat you out of life. I wish you could have known that. I know that I will forever be working on my ability to open up to others. After a lifetime of stowing away my feelings and secrets, I still find it difficult to divulge my thoughts to those closest to me. I will never deny my past because even though it put me through hell, I am who I am.

I truly wish that I could have been there to hold your hand or take you in my arms and tell you that you matter. I would let you know that the voices of pain and disappointment will begin to dwindle. I cannot ever promise that life will get better, but there is that glimmer of hope to reach out for in the darkness. You no longer physically exist, you are but a faint memory for myself, but not a day goes by that I do not think about you. For better or for worse, you are a memory that I will never let go of.

Never give up.

I am proud to say that I love you. I love who we are becoming, and I know you will too. That is the biggest step. Accepting who I am and no longer experiencing the suffocating sense of self-loathing. Try to smile. I know it hurts to hide your pain behind the mask that society wants to see, but just try it. Occasionally, smiling does make you feel better.

You deserve the world. You are capable of greatness.

Love,

Lauren

A Letter to My 18-Year-Old Self

by
Tara Goldstein

Dear Tara:

Happy 18th Birthday! It's November 14, 1975, and you're in the middle of your first semester at Marianapolis College, a private Anglophone CEGEP in Montreal. You're having a blast. Your favourite course is an introductory Women's Studies course with Christine Overall who will become a Professor in the Department of Philosophy at Queen's and hold a Queen's University Research Chair. Christine will have you read *The Second Sex* by Simone de Beauvoir, and after the class discussion on Beauvoir's argument that one is not born a woman but *becomes* a woman, life will never be the same again.

In 2011, at the age of 54 you will begin writing a play called *Castor and Sylvie*, which is about Simone de Beauvoir and her mid-life companion Sylvie Le Bon. You probably haven't heard of Sylvie Le Bon. But you will, once you start reading biographies about de Beauvoir written in the 1990s and 2000s. I know: the 1990s and 2000s seem very far away right now.

You may be wondering if you've become a playwright. You have. You will complete a MFA degree in Playwriting at Spalding University in Louisville, Kentucky, and become the Artistic Director of your own independent theatre company called Gailey Road Productions. The company will produce research-informed theatre on social and political issues that matter to us all, and its tagline will be "Where Theatre Meets Research and Research Meets Theatre". Pretty cool, eh?

You may be wondering why your theatre company is so interested in research. Well, in the mid-1980s you're going to go to graduate school at OISE at the University of Toronto and became an educational ethnographer interested in issues of equity in schooling. You know how much you're enjoying that anthropology course you're taking? Well, it turns out that you're going to have a life-long interest in anthropology.

You may be wondering why you're interested in writing a play about Simone de Beauvoir and Sylvie Le Bon. Well, the short answer is that the play is part of your **ongoing project of putting queer families on stage.**

Now you may be wondering why you're interested in staging the lives of queer families. You may even be wondering what a queer family is. And if you can kind of know what a queer family is, you may be wondering if it's okay to call that kind of family "queer". The only time you've ever heard the word queer used has been when its been used as an insult.

Okay. Maybe you had better sit down. Lots of things are going to change for you in about twenty years. Twenty years from now, you're going to go out to celebrate your 38th birthday with a friend named Margot and after the movie, during coffee, you're going to come out to her. As a lesbian. Don't freak out. It's not going to be as bad as you think. In twenty years from now peoples' attitudes towards lesbian, gay and bisexual folks will be much more open and accepting. You and Margot will start dating, move in together, buy a condo and get married. Both your families will attend the ceremony at City Hall, Mum will make centre pieces for the wedding dinner which you're holding at a lovely Italian restaurant in Toronto called Casa Mia and the only drama that day will come from not knowing that you had to bring the paperwork you filled out at City Hall six weeks earlier *with you* on the day you get married.

Yes, you'll have to rush home in a taxi to find the paperwork and bring it back down to City Hall while Margot, paler than you've ever seen her in the 14 years you've been together, tells both your families that the ceremony has to be postponed until you return. Yes, you're not sure that when you return with the paperwork 40 minutes later if the Marriage Officiant can squeeze you in between the other weddings that are taking place that evening. But don't worry. Everything will work out fine and in the end you'll have a pretty funny story to tell about the day you got married. I know that right now, none of this may seem very funny at all. But it will. Thirty-four years from now.

You may be wondering if you and Margot have kids. You don't, but you have 13 nephews and nieces between the two of you and you see most of them often. Carl and his family will settle down in Los Angeles and you won't see his three kids as often as the other nephews and nieces. But Carl's daughter Evyn-Rose, named after both of your grandmothers, will come to visit you and Margot and the rest of the family for a week to celebrate her 16th birthday. You'll take her to visit Ryerson where she can study Fashion Design. And if she decides to come to Toronto when she's 18, you'll have a wonderful opportunity to get to know her better.

I seem to have come full circle: from your own 18th year to your niece Evyn-Rose's 18th year. Every one of the years between your 18th birthday and Evyn-Rose's will be exciting in its own way. Not every moment is going to be easy. Finding your research question for your PhD thesis won't be much fun at all and the merger between the Faculty of Education at the University of Toronto where you get your first job and OISE where you graduated with your PhD will be even less fun. But you'll make it through the hard times and have the joy of reading this letter out to an audience of Gailey Road supporters during the fourth season of Women Writing Letters, a literary performance series that you start in 2011. The same year you begin *Castor and Sylvie*. Enjoy yourself on your 18th birthday.

Lots of love,
Tara, age 57

A Letter to My 18-Year-Old Self

by
Tanya Neumeyer

On Queer Literature: A Spoken Word Poem

I wish I'd grown up with queer stories
stories that help me trust new beginnings
that breakdown, dance with and redefine normal
stories that set me free

because the power of stories defines what can and cannot be
said
and being queer is not just about coming out
though being queer is still sometimes a news story
in contrast to the never headlining but ever present story that
kept me straight for so long
called heteronormativity
called "normal"
called all you hear about
the underbelly here is story as power

so if I could go back in time as a storyteller
I would say to my 18 year old self
tanya, little bright, shiny one
let me tell you a story about once upon a future time
when you will hear of a body of work called queer literature

perk up your ears
sit puppy dog, wide eyed, silent and soak it all in
when the time comes you must listen

these are stories that will heal you
by seeing you through the internalized tight tension and turmoil
that is homophobia

queer lit is fiction and non-fiction, stories of our people
that will help you find that shiny new queer life you will lead
but you don't know it yet
you have no clue
after all, no one's stopped to ask you
"when did you first decide that you were straight?"
with all the heterosexist narratives that make dictionary bound
people
that work to make you who you are for now
you wouldn't dare admit it, not for years

I want to tell you where you come from
where our people have been and what we have done
a whole history and herstory and transtories of LGBTQQ2SI heroes
to date
- ah, to date!
yes darling, but dating is another story

a book of lessons written just for you
through wide open eyes, from songs sung within
it begins with her lips, bares breasts and that whole body of work
that you learn
one intimate moment at a time

what you learn in dating you can't learn from literature
study both
study Anne-Marie MacDonald's Fall on Your Knees, Hejira
it will haunt you into your own desire

take notes on Tipping the Velvet, thank you Sarah Waters and the
BBC
a whole history of we-come-from-long-ago-too
tip head over heels in love the ladies in love with ladies

let the lyrics of Ani Difranco swoon you to sleep with sweetly
radical lullabyes
when the whole world of queer possibilities is too big to dance in
take rest but learn your history
Saphho is our mythology
ancient Greek and great-great-great-great-great-great-great-
great-great-grandmother

brazen femme written daily
as trans and gender queer people of our own definitions
create new encyclopaedias of ways to be
hear me say yes and
Anna Camerilli, Krystle Mullin, Truth Is, Andrea Gibson, Lishai Peel
and Barbara Erochina now
a whole new life long reading list
flashback to Audre Lorde and repeat
that powerhouse self-defined as "black, lesbian, mother, warrior,
poet"
come to ask if I'm doing my work
knows that fear does not protect us
instead we must speak, I speak
for those too threatened to speak of love and desire
for those boxed into definitions created systematically
by the culture of straight money and media
for queer heroes making their way in the world today
grand constellations of stars connecting stories
weaving bright light and whole lives out of threadbare
beginnings

contemporary queer lit will be written about you and I
if we burn down this house of fear and write a book
call it yes!
title it now
give it wings to take flight from the page
after volumes of experience, digested
there is power in telling our stories
and it sets us free

A Letter to My 18-Year-Old Self

by
Dryden Rainbow

Dear Dryden,

Let me start by saying your hair gets better.

I wanted to get that out of the way because once I tell you where I am writing from and who I am, there is a high probability that you will laugh, cry or faint. So here it is: I am writing to you from the future and I, in fact, am you. Albeit, you in four years time.

Now, to anyone else, I might say don't panic or quote Douglas Adams to give this letter some form of third person validation (if university has taught me anything, it's that I know nothing and it is better to quote someone who does). But, knowing you as I do, I would bet you have already crunched this letter into a small ball and thrown it into the corner of your predictably messy room. I completely understand the impulse; having watched an abundance of science fiction films, I know that intervening in the past almost never goes well for the protagonist and, furthermore, can have devastating ramifications. I know that writing this letter has the potential to initiate one or more temporal paradoxes including, but not limited to, the bootstrap, grandfather and predestination paradox. Even armed with this knowledge, I could not reasonably pass up the opportunity to talk to my younger self. So, hoping that you either did not crumple up this letter or you rescued it from the corner of your room where things go to die, I shall continue.

However, as it turns out, these things are not so easy to write. Like wedding vows, valedictorian speeches, and essays pertaining to the merits of democracy. What can I say — or write — that hasn't been said plenty of times before? And by someone more educated and more eloquent? What exactly does a 22-year-old student who doesn't pay her own rent say to an 18-year-old server who lives at home?

I suppose what I've got is the power of hindsight. And so, at first, I thought I should tell you the winning lottery numbers or the outcome of the next four years' Super Bowls. But, I worry that giving you such information would, potentially, incite a butterfly effect situation wherein something I say leads to the toppling of a state government that is already in a precarious position. Thus, this letter will not be chalk full of advice on how to invest your money, who to bet on to win the Stanley Cup (though I do feel confident telling you it will not be the Leafs), or how to style your hair.

I also hesitate to tell you too much about where you end up in four years. Honestly, who knows if your life will end up anything like mine. One thing, this letter even, could completely change the path of your life. Furthermore, if your life does end up resembling mine, I don't want to risk jeopardizing it or ruining the surprise that awaits you.

And so, here we are.

Having exhausted my initial list of ideas, I turned to my reliable friend who always has the answers in times of crisis: Google. After typing, "Writing a letter to yourself," I was greeted by over 67 million results. As it turns out, a lot of people want to write letters to themselves and have no idea how to do it. Thankfully, Google has a lot to say on the topic. Cindy Crawford even weighs in.

If given the chance, Cindy Crawford would tell a younger version of herself: you're good enough and you should probably have more fun.

Pretty good advice.

Turns out, Cindy Crawford is not the only celebrity that has contemplated the question. Shirley MacLaine would tell her younger self to eat less sugar whereas Whoopi Goldberg would say: stay out of your own way.

After making my way through pages of Google searches, I realized most posts shared one salient trait: if you are lucky enough to speak to a younger version of yourself, use the opportunity to share a piece of advice. While this may sound simple, finding that one piece of advice that is worth risking a temporal paradox, is anything but.

However, then I stumbled upon a letter written by a woman named Wendy. She used her letter to tell her younger self something she needed to know, something she likely *already* knew, but was unable or unwilling to vocalize and confront. This was a sentiment I could relate to. I, you, we (there is an inherent pronoun problem in writing a letter to yourself) have a tendency to ignore things until they crystallize into something heavy, a weight we carry around like a tumour.

So, the moment you have been waiting for: my piece of advice. It is not new, poetic, highbrow or revolutionary. There is a strong likelihood that it stems from a beauty advertisement. Nonetheless, here it is: let yourself be loved.

I know, it sounds like a *L'Oréal Paris* commercial. But, even if it's a tagline used to sell cosmetics, it's still pertinent. It might also seem a tad ridiculous—who refuses to let themselves be loved? As it turns out, we do.

In addition to your hair, there are lots of things that you get a handle on in the next four years: high-waisted shorts, cartwheels, whistling obnoxiously at sporting events. But, there are a good many that you are still utterly confused about. Like semicolons, politics in the Middle East, and relationships—romantic and otherwise.

As the daughter of a single mother and, later, a member of a blended family with enough sibling drama to inspire at least four solid seasons of *Young and the Restless*, relationships became an issue of resources. More specifically, of learning not to demand them. There was always something else, someone else, who required the attention of people in our life and thus, we learned not to be a burden. Always the Virgo. Don't misunderstand my meaning: it's not that you (we) don't want love or that love can only be expressed in the form of attention. Although I'm sure you already know all this. You are, after all, living the same life I did.

What you don't know is this quality only magnifies in university. Thrown into a new environment, you figure the best way to make friends and win people over is to be a net positive in their lives. You do this by finding ways to benefit their lives and demanding nothing in return. For example, you become everyone's go-to editor, reading boring essays on topics like International Political Economy and whether the United States should use unmanned aerial vehicles. Spoiler Alert: there's no good answer to that question.

This quality, a sort of selflessness, is not a bad thing. In fact, it's something parents are eager to teach their children. But, your motivation for doing it and what it means for the relationships you build is, quite frankly, not great. It comes from a place of fear and crippling insecurity. Of believing that if you lean on another, they will no longer see your worth and leave. So, you go out of your way to make sure no one has reason to question your value. On top of this, you have a tendency to keep people at arm's length out of a fear of them seeing you vulnerable and deciding you're not worth the effort. But you are. You are worth the effort. And thinking you're not — thinking I'm not — does everyone a disservice. You do not need to prove your value or fear needing others. Give the people in your life the benefit of the doubt.

I say this, not because I've figured it out, but because I haven't. I realize it might seem like odd advice, but in four years' time when you finish university and you're desperately trying to translate the friendships you've made into something sustainable, this will be the thing stopping you from doing so. I hope this letter gives you (me, us) a head start in working it out.

So, there it is. Jump off the swing-set and let yourself be loved.

With high hopes,

Dryden

WRITERS' BIOGRAPHIES

SHIRLEY BARRIE is a playwright who also used to be an artistic director/producer. She co-founded the Wakefield Tricycle Company, now the Tricycle Theatre in London, England, and Straight Stitching Productions in Toronto, and received two Chalmers and a Dora Award for *Straight Stitching* and *Carrying the Calf*. In the last ten years she returned to her early roots in music theatre with *Hansel and Gretel,* for Geordie Productions in Montreal, *Bozo's Fortune,* an adaptation of Puccini's *Gianni Schicchi* that toured schools with Shoestring Opera, and two plays for 4th Line Theatre: *Beautiful Lady, Tell Me…,* a vaudevillian, musical murder mystery, and *Queen Marie* – the story of the Cobourg born great comic actress, Marie Dressler. She also writes plays without music. *Measure of the World,* about scientific discovery, espionage and ego, was produced as part of the inaugural Fireworks Festival of New Plays at the Alumnae Theatre in 2013, and the Alumnae will be producing *I am Marguerite* on their main stage in April of 2015. Shirley is also writing another play for 4th Line about L.M. Montgomery's years in Leaskdale Ontario.

GAIL BENICK is a professor in the humanities at Sheridan College in Oakville, Ontario. Her area of specialization is immigration, diaspora and storytelling. In addition to her academic publications, she is a creative writer with a story recently appearing in Jewish.Fiction.net and another forthcoming in Parchment. Her debut novel, *The Girl Who Was Born That Way*, will be published by Inanna Publications in 2015.

LOUISE BOLTBEE divides her time between her role as coordinator at The Listening Centre and working as an artist's model for various colleges, universities and artists' groups in the city. In her spare time she works on a family of graphic designs printed on t-shirts, aprons and onesies for babies as featured on her website allthatiam.com. Recently she has also dedicated her creative energy to designing a line of scarves featuring excerpts from her writings. It was back in elementary school, grade 4 in fact, when she realized something inside of her wanted to write and tell stories. Since then she has been filling the pages of her journals with poems, prose and children's stories. She wishes to thank 'Women Writing Letters' for this wonderful opportunity to share with others her love of writing and storytelling. Writing a "Letter to Your Grandmother", she says, has been a remarkable experience.

JOAN BURROWS is a retired English and Dramatic Arts teacher who has turned to playwriting as a second career. Her plays include: *Staff Room* (Theatre Ontario Winner, 2004 and published by Canada Playwrights Press in *Grassroots* 2011); *The Photograph* (ACT-CO award winner in 2008; staged reading at Theatrestarts 2012); *Willow Quartet* (Playwrights of Spring Winner, 2009) and *Gloria's Guy* (staged at the New Ideas Festival, Alumnae Theatre 2012). Besides playwriting, Joan has been an active volunteer with TAPA – Toronto Alliance for the Performing Arts – for the last 10 years and has Chaired the Independent Jurors for the Dora Mavor Moore Awards.

KAYE CARONONGAN is currently in her fourth-year as an undergraduate student at the University of Toronto, double majoring in Equity Studies and Philosophy. She says that if she had to describe herself in one way, it would be that motivating people gives her a high. Here's a quote from Kaye: "There's something about seeing someone smile that makes me come alive. You can see it in their eyes and feel it in their spirit's presence. It's very humbling. Or perhaps they're just patiently standing in front of me, subliminally telling me to shove off their spot before their class starts in 5 minutes."

ELIZABETH CINELLO is a Toronto-based writer, cultural animator, and community activist. She is a co-founder of Art Starts Neighbourhood Cultural Centre. In addition to multidisciplinary theatrical productions and audience participatory events, her work includes installations, video documentaries, and community-based projects. Elizabeth writes short stories as well as articles and travel pieces about culture and city life. She is a regular contributor to Living Toronto Journal, an on-line publication about living in the city. Her popular short story, "Food Companion Wanted", winner of *Accenti Magazine*'s 2011 Short

Story Contest, has been translated into Italian, anthologized, and she performed in storytelling festivals.

JEN COOK is a passionate singer and voice teacher. Her desire to sing and teach is born out of her belief that sharing our life experience through songs and stories is essential to the evolution of one's spiritual, mental and physical self. Jen has worked as an actor both on and off camera, has written, performed and produced cabarets, solo shows and has sung in intimate venues around the city. From her studio in downtown Toronto, she works with professional singers, actors, public speakers and the "I've always wanted to sing' crowd".

KATRINA COOK is a grade 12 student who started the Gay-Straight Alliance at her school four years ago. She is a guitar playing rocker and chorister. She identifies as queerspawn and bisexual, and comes from a long line of bisexuals. Her published writing includes the personal essay "'Shut Up' Or Why I Ended Up in the Hall".

BEVERLEY COOPER has written for TV, film and extensively for CBC radio drama, and was twice being nominated for Writers' Guild of Canada Awards. Her plays include *Thin Ice* (co-written with Banuta Rubess), *The Eyes of Heaven*, *The Woman in White* (adapted from the novel by Wilkie Collins) and *The Lonely Diner: Al Capone in Euphemia Township*. Beverley's play, *Innocence Lost: A Play about Steven Truscott* was a finalist for the Governor General's Literary Award and on the Globe and Mail bestseller list, a first for a Canadian playwright. Beverley recently completed her MFA in Creative Writing at the University of Guelph.

FARZANA DOCTOR is a novelist and psychotherapist. Her most recent novel *Six Metres of Pavement* was named one of *Now Magazine*'s Top Ten Books of 2011. It also won the Lambda Literary prize and was short-listed for the Toronto Book Award. She is currently finishing her third novel and co-curates the Brockton Writers Series. www.farzanadoctor.com

ANN EYERMAN is the author of *Mediterranean Journey: A Young Woman's Travels Through 1970s Europe* -- a collection of seven stories loosely based on her own journeys. She is also the author of *Women in the Office: Transitions in a Global Economy* (Sumach

Press, 2000), and "Serving Up Service: Fast Food and Office Workers Doing It with a Smile," in *Women Working the NAFTA Food Chain: Women, Food & Globalization* edited by Deborah Barndt (Second Story Press, 1999). Ann was also a contributor to *Women Writing Letters, Season 2, Celebrating the Art.* In November, 2014, she appeared with four other artists as part of Writes of Passage: Love and a Sense of Place at the Windup Bird Cafe. Ann lives in Toronto where she works as job coach, writer, Excellent Cat Sitter and blogger. She lives with two rescued cats, who have become regular contributors to her blog, Annie's Odyssey (http://anneyerman.wordpress.com/).

CLARRIE FEINSTEIN is a second year undergraduate student currently majoring in English and minoring in History and Drama at the University of Toronto. In 2013-2014 Clarrie took the Creative Writing course offered at Victoria College and participated in the Playwriting class. As an aspiring writer and an ardent reader, Women Writing Letters provided the perfect opportunity to begin a future of reading works written by herself. There is nothing like the ideals of youth. Clarrie also dabbles in music. Having played the cello and having trained in classical voice, she is now learning some chords on the ukulele. She is currently a writer for the U of T independent paper called *The Newspaper* performed in Trinity College's musical *Into the Woods* in 2014. Clarrie loves to travel and believes that that has been her most valuable education, an education, which her supportive and loving parents have given her the privilege to enjoy.

STACY GARDNER is a writer of poetry, plays and short stories. The latter she has been more earnest about recently. Stacy's poem 'A Place of Origin' was published in 2012 in Toronto's: *City Voices, a book of monologues and poems.* Her short play *Worms for Sale,* in which she had the pleasure of working with Bev Cooper as her script editor, was originally commissioned by CBC radio, then later adapted and staged with Alumnae Theatre. Alumnae Theatre has invited Stacy to write the *Worms for Sale* as a full-length play and they are looking at the possibility of a production in November 2015. As of late, Stacy has been dusting off much poetry, and sending it out into The Universe. A winner of the Columbia Scholastic Press Association in NYC for Non-Fiction, Stacy's article 'Into the Abyss', examined Post Traumatic Stress Disorder in journalists. Stacy's inspiration is often stoked by human interest stories and social justice issues. Stacy's background in social services, especially with the young people at Covenant House Toronto, a sacred source of grounding and love. Stacy created, Quills on the Edge, a writing and performance workshop for at-risk youth in Toronto. Having recently moved to St. John's, NL, Stacy has carried the mission with her, and is now facilitating in Newfoundland. She lives there with her partner and their 3-year-old son, Cohen.

LAUREN GILLIES is currently in her fourth year as an undergraduate student at the University of Toronto. She is completing a double major in cinema studies and drama, which are two of her passions. Lauren has performed in multiple campus shows with the Trinity College Dramatic Society including *Spring Awakening*, *The Frogs*, and *Into the Woods*. She has completed internships for OUTtv and Convergent Productions, as a marketing and branding assistant, as well as a production assistant. Lauren is thrilled to be a part of this collection, and thanks everyone involved.

JOAN GREEN is an educator who has made a significant impact on education over the course of her career. In 1990, she became the first woman CEO and Director of the Toronto Board of Education. She is also the Founding CEO of Ontario's Education Quality and Accountability Office (EQAO), which is dedicated to increasing the success of students and the quality of education across the province. Joan is an outspoken advocate for equity and diversity. She has organized student food programs and educational bursaries for teenaged mothers, spearheaded province-wide awareness of organ donation, and has published on and spoken both nationally and internationally on leadership, assessment, equity issues, and curricula. In honour of her exceptional contributions to education in Ontario, Joan was appointed to the Order of Ontario, the province's highest honour, on February 6, 2013.

AMANDA GREER is an undergraduate student at the University of Toronto, Trinity College, double majoring in English and Cinema Studies. She recently worked as an Event Co-ordinator and Communications Assistant for Women in Film & Televeision-Toronto, contributing to the organization's efforts to create opportunities and support systems for women working in the film and television industries. She has also worked as an Editorial Intern and Assistant Video Producer at Trend Hunter Magazine, publishing over 850 articles. A member of the Trinity College Dramatic Society, Amanda has performed in several dramatic productions, most notably *Into the Woods*, for which she received the U of T Drama Coalition Award for Best Leading Actress in a Musical. She is also the Food Columnist and Communications Co-ordinator for Trinity's magazine, *The Salterrae*. She hopes to attend graduate school for Cinema Studies researching representations of women on-screen.

MARCIA JOHNSON is an actor, playwright and librettist. She also teaches an introduction to playwriting course in the prestigious music theatre department at Sheridan College. Marcia is the former Chair of the Playwrights Guild of Canada Women's Caucus and the current Vice President of Women Playwrights International. Tara first got to know Marcia at the Women Playwrights International Conference in Mumbai where she presented her play *Say Ginger Ale*. The play was subsequently produced at the 2010 SummerWorks Festival. Other plays include *Late* (Obsidian Theatre Company), *Courting Johanna* (Blyth Festival), and *Binti's Journey* (Theatre Direct Canada). Recently Marcia has published her play *Linden's Sister* in the collection *More than a Play* (Elementary Teachers' Federation of Ontario) and a short version of her play *Late* in *Give Voice: Ten Twenty Minute Plays from the Obsidian Theatre Company Playwrights Unit*. Marcia's first full-length opera *Paradises Lost* with composer Stephen A. Taylor was staged at the University of Illinois, Champaign-Urbana in April 2012 and performed in Toronto at the 2013 Summer Works Festival.

JO LAMPERT is an academic and writer who directs a large teacher education program for high poverty schools in Brisbane, Queensland, Australia. Born in Toronto, she has lived in Brisbane, for nearly twenty years, and is confused and divided about her sense of home.

JOANNE LATIMER is an actor, director and teacher in the Toronto area. A member of Actors' Equity and Actra, she has performed theatrically in and around Toronto including Second City, and New York, recently playing the role of Harriet in Gailey Road's production of *Harriet's House*. She has also appeared in film and television including the George F. Walker series *Living in Your Car* and numerous television commercials. She has taught English and Drama in Toronto for twenty years and has directed teenagers in numerous productions for stage, ranging from Shakespeare to contemporary works to original collaborative creations. She is continually recharged by the creative energy and authenticity that her students bring to the work. Joanne is also committed to equity issues in the school environment and has been involved in the school's staff and student equity committees. Joanne's other interests include writing and music. She has served as a literary editor for Eddy Press. She plays guitar and sings, often performing acoustically at local venues, and is currently singing in a rock/blues cover band. An advocate of lifelong learning, Joanne continues to take classes in acting, singing and, most recently, earned a diploma from the Basic Actor Intensive course in stage combat from Rapier Wit in Toronto.

SARAH LEVY is currently a third year student at Trinity College at the University of Toronto, and is pursuing a double major in Ethics, Society, and Law and Environmental Studies. Sarah is from Winnipeg, Manitoba and attended St. John's Ravenscourt School, where she devoted her high school years to debating. Sarah was excited to be a part of the Women Writing Letters event, as she has always had a passion for both creative writing and public speaking. Apart from writing, Sarah's other interests include reading, painting, travelling, hiking, and spending time with animals. She is passionate about conservation, and is serving as the current President of the Trinity College Environmental Society. Sarah is also working as an Eco-Journalist at the University of Toronto Sustainability Office. After graduating, Sarah is hoping to crew with the Sea Shepherd Conservation Society before pursuing a degree in Environmental Law.

MARY ELLEN MACLEAN is a performer, creator, and director originally from Nova Scotia. She was a founding member of the Halifax physical theatre ensemble, *Jest in Time*, with whom she toured worldwide for twenty years. The company also starred in three national CBC television specials. Mary Ellen's one-woman play *Frankie* toured across Canada and aired on Bravo TV for the Singular Series. Her movement play *Velocipede*, using twenty-one bicycles, seven dancers/actresses played to sold out audiences. Mary Ellen works across the country as a director and a performer. She also teaches theatre, movement and improvisation throughout the year to people of all ages. Nova

170

Scotia Merritt Theatre Awards include: Twenty Years of Theatre Excellence *(Jest in Time)*; Best Production (*Trip-Jest*); nominations for Best New Play *(Frankie)*, Best Actress *(Trip, Frankie)*. In the spring of 2015 Mary Ellen will be performing in *Emily's Piano* at Young People's Theatre where she is also developing a play about dyslexia entitled *Imagine a Lifetime*. Mary Ellen is a hockey player and collector of old bicycles.

TANYA NEUMEYER is a queer poet and educator. As a member of the League of Canadian Poets and the Toronto Poetry Project, Tanya performs poetry and offers workshops at festivals, conferences, events and schools across Ontario. In the 2014-2015 school year Tanya is part of the Ontario Arts Council's Artist in Education program. As a member of the 2012 Toronto Poetry Slam team that placed third in the country and competed internationally, Tanya brings a wealth of performing experience to a stage or classroom.

ALICIA PAYNE is a professional actor, published writer and an artist educator. Her credits encompass theatre, film, television and radio and her professional memberships include ACTRA, CAEA, Dramatists Guild of America and Playwrights Guild of Canada. Alicia is an alumna of the Playwrights Collective at Theatre Passe Muraille and the Tapestry Opera Composer Librettist Laboratory. She's also a co-founder of Arbez Drama Projects, a playwright-driven theatre company. A reading of *Justice for Maurice Henry Carter*, co-written with Donald Molnar, was part of the Readers' Theatre of New Works at the 2013 National Black Theatre Festival in North Carolina. Alicia is a contributor to the *Encyclopedia of African American Music* and is currently writing the libretto for a project about Canadian Forces Families.

KARLEEN PENDLETON JIMÉNEZ is a writer, professor and butch mama. She is the daughter of a progressive feminine mother, and a suburban Dad who wears dresses around strip malls. Karleen is cousin to two lesbianish women and a gay Russian interpreter, she has a stepson who likes the colour pink, a bisexual step-daughter, and a little princess girl. She has published numerous queer personal essays, a film called *Tomboy*, and two books *Are You a Boy or a Girl?* and *How to Get a Girl Pregnant*.

CAROLYN PETERS was born and raised in Toronto. She attended three public schools, two high schools, two universities and one college. With more than 30 years' experience, both as a student and as a teacher, Carolyn was well qualified to write A Letter to the Teacher I'll Never Forget. After working as an Interior Designer, a teacher and an owner of several businesses, Carolyn decided to go back to school, once again. She finally found a position where she could use her left brain and right brain, in equal proportions. She was hired as a middle manager in a downtown hospital. When she told her son about her new job, he said she had found her perfect job: a job where she could "talk on the phone all day and get paid for it". Working in the hospital has afforded Carolyn many opportunities to explore new avenues and experiences. However, when her mother was diagnosed with Alzheimer's, Carolyn decided to take early retirement. Finding herself at home with her mother, Carolyn has spent her "spare time" designing jewelry, writing short stories and doing genealogical research. When a friend asked Carolyn how she liked retirement she said, "I get to do anything I want and I can't get fired."

HELEN PICARD is a Toronto native. Her poetry has been published by several magazines such as Catfish Creek, Talking Soup Magazine, and Calliope Magazine. She hopes to one day pursue a Masters of Fine Arts in Creative Writing.

DRYDEN RAINBOW is a fourth year student at the University of Toronto majoring in Political Science and Cinema Studies. She has been involved in a variety of activities both on and off campus, including: three terms as secretary of Trinity College's Non-Resident Affairs Committee, contributor to student publications The Salterrae and The Varsity, a volunteer at Regent Park's Community Centre for Leaning and Development and Big Brothers and Sisters of Halton. Dryden is passionate about movies, local politics, analog photography, and live music. Though she has no immediate plans upon completion of her undergraduate degree, she wants to work and travel. Her goals include finding the perfect flannel shirt, learning to jump off a swing set, traveling Canada from coast-to-coast, and finding a way to make her hair look good the moment she gets out of bed.

SHELLY SANDERS is the author of three historical fiction novels, Rachel's Secret, Rachel's Promise and most recently Rachel's

Hope, published by Second Story Press. Together, these books are The Rachel Trilogy, which has received Starred Reviews in *Booklist* and *CM Magazine*, and *Rachel's Secret* was an iTunes Book of the Week. *Rachel's Secret* and *Rachel's Hope* have also been distinguished as Notable Books by the Association of Jewish Libraries. Shelly has been chosen to be a Touring Author with TD Canada Book Week 2015, and will be travelling throughout Manitoba in May presenting her books. Before turning to fiction, Shelly worked as a freelance writer for 20 years with articles in *Maclean's, Toronto Star, National Post, Canadian Living*, and *Reader's Digest*. Shelly lives in Oakville with her husband, three children, two dogs and two lizards. Her oldest daughter, Amanda, is in her fourth year at Trinity College U of T, and has enjoyed working on Women Writing Letters with Tara over the past two years.

GILLIAN SCOTT is a third year undergraduate at Trinity College at the University of Toronto, majoring in Classics and Classical Civilizations. When she isn't studying languages that no one speaks anymore, she enjoys acting, sleeping, and reading cheesy teen novels.

JOSÉE SIGOUIN was born in Montréal, lived in the national capital through her teens and has since made a home in Toronto. She is an aspiring novelist, a founding member of the literary critique group, First Page, and past finalist for the Penguin Random House of Canada Student Award for Fiction. She works at the University of Toronto where she once served as the Status of Women Officer. More recently she keeps busy meeting the challenges of data analysis on the state of university research—massaging numbers to tell factual stories by day and massaging words to tell fictional ones by night. She is writing a first novel, *The Fifth Season*.

KARINE SILVERWOMAN is an artist, counselor, educator, personal trainer and community minded activist. Her art practice includes poetry, video and dance. Her award-winning video *Hello, My Name is Herman* has screened internationally and her work has been published in *No More Potlucks Magazine* and *Shameless Magazine*. She received the Karol Steinhouse award for demonstrating commitment to issues of social justice as they relate to sexual orientation, gender and diversity. She has her Masters in Social Work from Ryerson and has worked at

Sherbourne Health Centre for several years. She is currently on maternity leave.

EMMA SMITH is double majoring in Ethics, Society, and Law and the Literary Criticism, Cultural Theory Stream at the University of Toronto. She is currently a staff writer for the *Salterrae*, Trinity College's quarterly magazine. She has an avid interest in the performing arts and will be performing the part of Cinderella in *Into the Woods* this March with the Trinity College Drama Society. She has worked as an actress, tutor, dance teacher, waitress, and even a Disney princess at birthday parties. She has volunteered at seniors' residences and the hospital in her hometown of Oakville and she has often fundraised for the Canadian Cancer Society. Emma is also a supporter of "Take Back the Night" and has spoken and performed at rallies on numerous occasions. Emma was very happy to be a part of Women Writing Letters and is Gailey Road's most recent Communication Assistant.

DIANA TSO is a performer, playwright, poet and storyteller who has worked with diverse theatres internationally for over 15 years. Diana graduated from the University of Toronto, in English Literature, and from Ecole Internationale de Théâtre de Jacques Lecoq, in Paris, France. Her theatre plays as co-creator include *and by the way Miss*...with Urge and Theatre Direct with whom she shares the Dora Mavor Moore award for outstanding ensemble performance and *Dante's Inferno* and *Chekhov Shorts* with Theatre Smith-Gilmour. Her recent play *Red Snow* premiered in 2012 in Toronto and at the Shanghai International Contemporary Theatre Festival. Diana is the artistic director of Red Snow Collective *www.redsnowcollective.ca* whose theatre vision merges east and west storytelling art forms through music, movement & text. *Red Snow* is love story inspired by the survivors of the Rape of Nanking 1937. Diana is now writing her first opera, *Peonies in Winter*. As well she is in development for her play, *Monkey Queen, journey to the East* which she currently shares as a storyteller in schools and festivals since its premiere at the 2010 Toronto Storytelling Festival.

SAMANTHA VAKIENER will graduate from Spalding University's MFA Program in Creative Writing this fall. Her focus is in play writing and she has many scripts in the works. She hails from Rochester, New York.

EDITORS' BIOGRAPHIES

TARA GOLDSTEIN is a professor and playwright in the Department of Curriculum, Teaching and Learning at the Ontario Institute of Studies in Education, University of Toronto. She is also the Founding Director of Gailey Road Productions, a theatre company that produces research-informed theatre on social and political issues that affect us all (www.gaileyroad.com). Tara has been writing and producing research-informed for thirteen years and has written about her work in *Staging Harriet's House: Writing and Producing Research-Informed Theatre* (Peter Lang 2012). Three of her research-informed plays appear in the anthology *Zero Tolerance and Other Plays: Disrupting Xenophobia, Racism and Homophobia at School* (Sense Publishers 2013). Tara's latest play *Castor and Sylvie* is a play about French feminist philosopher Simone de Beauvoir and her companion philosophy teacher Sylvie Le Bon. Tara also curates *Women Writing Letters*, a fundraising literary event for Gailey Road that takes place four times a year. *Women Writing Letters* is in its fourth season.

AMANDA GREER is an undergraduate student at the University of Toronto, Trinity College, double majoring in English and Cinema Studies. She recently worked as an Event Co-ordinator and Communications Assistant for Women in Film & Televeision-Toronto, contributing to the organization's efforts to create opportunities and support systems for women working in the film and television industries. She has also worked as an Editorial Intern and Assistant Video Producer at Trend Hunter Magazine, publishing over 850 articles. A member of the Trinity College Dramatic Society, Amanda has performed in several dramatic productions, most notably *Into the Woods*, for which she received the U of T Drama Coalition Award for Best Leading Actress in a Musical. She is also the Food Columnist and Communications Co-ordinator for Trinity's magazine, *The Salterrae*. She hopes to attend graduate school for Cinema Studies researching representations of women on-screen.